PROOF OF DEATH

ST. MARIN'S COZY MYSTERY SERIES - BOOK 7

ACF BOOKENS

1

I f I hadn't owned a bookstore, I'd probably have become a librarian. I loved books that much. Today was my weekly day off from my own bookstore, All Booked Up, and while I had luxurious plans to prepare my garden spot and maybe even get a few seeds in the ground, I was now at the library.

Basically, my trip into town for breakfast tacos at Lu's truck had gone a bit awry when I'd needed to avoid Max, a man I had been sort of dating, a little, maybe . . . for a bit but now just didn't want to date at all. I hadn't yet told him that because, to be honest, I was a coward. We hadn't really even gotten started, but what we had done was flirt a lot and I wasn't really ready yet to flirt with anyone. Not after my last break up. Rebounds were brutal, and I needed to tell Max where we stood. But like I said, a coward.

So when I'd seen him coming up the street toward the taco truck, I had ducked down a side-street only to come upon the library on the day of their annual book sale. I did not need any books. I had a whole store full of them, for goodness sakes, but I don't know any true bibliophile who can resist a library book sale. After all, the proceeds do two acts of good – they get us books, and they help other people get books.

Thus, there I was inside amongst long folding tables full of boxes of books that were loosely grouped by genre. I'd been thinking about reading more thrillers lately, inspired by the police officer who leads a thriller book group in one of my favorite books, *The Storied Life of AJ Fikry*, and so I was trying to figure out which Mark Dawson book was the first in his Beatrix Rose series when two of my favorite people in the world, Stephen and Walter Hitchcock-Arritt, stopped across the table from me and stared until I looked up from the back cover I was reading.

"Oh good, we thought you'd fallen asleep with your eyes open," Stephen said. "That good, huh?"

I rolled my eyes. "Actually, I'm just confused." I held up *The Dragon and the Ghost* and *The Angel*. "Mother or daughter?"

"Mother, of course. Go with the original," Walter answered without hesitation. "Then, you can look forward to seeing if her daughter is as bad-ass as she is."

I smiled. "And you like to pretend you're all high culture. Clearly, you've read these." I gestured toward the ten titles I'd laid out in front of me. "Maybe I should just get them all?"

Stephen picked up a paper bag from a stack nearby, came around the table, and dropped all ten Dawson books in the bag. "It's a whole bag of mass markets for three dollars. Go wild, Harvey."

I laughed and dropped in a few more titles before following my friends toward the counter to pay. "You two here for a bargain? Or were you detoured from tacos by your own cowardice, too?"

Stephen winced. "Still avoiding Max?" He sighed. "Do you want me to tell him?"

Walter and I both shouted "No!" at the same time and then cringed when every eye in the not-so-quiet library turned toward us. I raised a hand of apology and then turned to Stephen. "This is not seventh grade. I can break up with my own boyfriends, thank you very much."

"So he *was* your boyfriend?" Stephen said. "Does he know that?"

I dropped my bag on the counter, pulled a five out of my wallet and told the teenager behind the desk to keep the change. Then, I turned to Stephen and stuck out my tongue. Clearly, this wasn't seventh grade; it was second.

Once the men had paid, I pointed toward a back corner. "Feel like pretending we're back in college and having a study group so we can gossip?" I was all about regressing apparently.

They looked at each other. I knew Stephen was always game for a good story, but Walter could be more a "take the high road" guy. Today, though, he must have either wanted a good tale or saw something desperate in my expression because he smiled and led the way back.

I picked up the conversation about Max as soon as we all sat down. "That's part of the problem. We hadn't really had a discussion about what we were to each other, so I don't want to presume that he was thinking we were dating, if he wasn't. But if he was, then I definitely need to say something official, right?"

Walter sighed. "Did you go on a date? Like where he took you somewhere other than his restaurant?"

I shook my head.

"Did he ask you if you'd like to 'go steady' or whatever people say these days?" Stephen asked.

I shook my head.

"Did you sleep with him?" Walter asked with a big smile.

"No, of course not." I sighed. "Okay, so we weren't dating. But then, how do I tell him that I don't even want to continue what we didn't really start?" This had been bugging me, and I really hoped my friends could give me advice. They'd been married for eight years and had dated six before that. They were the most solid couple I knew besides my parents, and I needed their wisdom.

Stephen took my hand. "When was the last time you talked to him?"

I sat back in the chair and thought. "Three weeks, maybe."

Walter laughed so loudly that a toddler in the children's section next door shushed him. "He knows, Harvey. You don't have to say anything."

"Oh, but that feels rude," I said.

This time, Stephen's cackle actually echoed. "Ruder than not talking to him for three weeks. His restaurant is just up the street from your store. You can't possibly think he'll consider it coincidence, do you?"

I blushed and felt my throat tighten. "When you put it like that . . ."

"It's fine, Harvey. Just stop avoiding him. Treat him like a friend, and it'll all be normal soon." Walter stood and took my hand. "Now, come help me pick out some large print mysteries for our neighbor. He's on a budget, but he loves books. I come every Saturday to get a few for him."

We wandered the tables that stretched across all the more open spaces of the library, and in the mystery section, I loaded Walter's arms with large print titles that I thought his neighbor would love given his preference for traditional mysteries. We found a real boon when I saw the entire set of Hamish MacBeth books by M.C. Beaton. "He'll love these. They're quaint and fun, but not too cozy or soft," I said.

"And no violence. He says he's had enough of that in his life," Stephen said as he joined us, his own stack of titles under one arm.

"Nope, no violence." I smiled and dropped the rest of the titles into Walter's bag. "I just want to go see what they have in nonfiction. I've been craving a great nature book. Meet you at the counter?"

The two men nodded as I moved toward the quiet front corner of the stacks where the nonfiction books were shelved and the titles for sale were set out accordingly. No one else was back there, which wasn't surprising. Just like in my shop, and probably in every book space in the world, people were almost always most interested in romances, thrillers, mysteries, and fantasy books. Nonfiction got the attention of some readers, especially if they wanted to learn a about a particular subject, and some readers only picked up nonfiction because they didn't find the escape into a fictional world to be their cup of tea. But far more people read tons more fiction than nonfiction. It was simply the way of readers.

Mostly, I was a fiction reader, too. I loved to disappear into a world I didn't know for myself or tag along with a character who navigated something like my life but in a whole new way. From time to time, though, I did want something that stayed in the world I knew, even if I'd never experienced it for myself. But I wanted more than just information. I wanted to be swept up in the language. Creative nonfiction usually did that for me, and so I scanned the boxes on the tables for titles by Tracy Kidder or Mary Roach, two of my favorite authors.

I was just reaching for a title by Erik Larsen, *Devil in the White City*, when I tripped over something on the floor. I stepped back and bent down, expecting to see a box of books. Instead, I saw a foot in a well-worn brown loafer.

When I bent further and looked under the table, the very still face of a man stared up at the table above him. He was about fifty with a pinkish complexion and an impressive walrus-style moustache. He wore khaki trousers and a sweater vest over a white, button-down shirt. If I hadn't already recognized him, the outfit alone might have made me guess he was a librarian.

He was, in fact, the head librarian, Sidney Scott. I'd known him ever since I moved to St. Marin's. He'd been pleasant enough to me, but he had a reputation for being kind of a dictator when it came to library fines and book condition. A customer once told me he demanded payment from a toddler who returned a board book that had peanut butter on it. He wasn't everyone's favorite person.

I got down on my hands and knees and crawled up to his face, but I could already tell he was dead. He wasn't breathing, and when I checked for his pulse, I didn't find one. I made my way back out from under the table and sat on the floor for a minute to get my head straight.

I stifled my impulse to shout for help both because I didn't want to have a crowd gathered around the man's body and because the rules of quiet in the library were engrained in me. I didn't want to leave the body either. I didn't see any signs of foul-play, but I'd unfortunately come upon enough bodies to know that looks could be deceiving. Plus, if he'd just had a heart attack or something, he'd have fallen into the middle of the library floor, not stuffed himself under the table.

Quickly, I texted Walter and Stephen and asked them to let the librarians know there'd been an accident in the nonfiction section. "Then come, please."

My friends were there in seconds, and as soon as they saw my face and Sidney's feet, they blanched. "He's dead?" Stephen asked as he sat down beside me and put his arm around my shoulders.

"Dead for sure." I sighed and then dialed the sheriff. "Tuck, we need you at the library. Sidney Scott is dead."

WHEN SHERIFF MASON TUCKER arrived a few minutes later, I was sitting at a table near the front counter with a cup of hot tea that one of the librarians had brought me. Walter had offered to stand guard near the body just to keep unsuspecting patrons from wandering over. He made up some story about a water leak to keep them away.

Mindy Washington, the young librarian who was, unexpectedly, now in charge, had made a quick decision to allow everyone in the library to stay so as to avoid panic or too much gossip, but she'd asked the children's librarian, Lucy, to lock the doors and linger nearby to let patrons out without a fuss. I thought that was a stellar idea.

I adored Mindy, partially because she seemed to love books as much as I did but also because she had this quirky sense of style that I kind of wanted to copy and might have but I feared that a middle-aged white lady with wild hair might not be able to pull off the sleek but unique look of a twenty-five-year-old black woman. Today, she was wearing wide-legged trousers with a silk floral blouse in many shades of pink, but instead of dress shoes, she had on pink Converse sneakers. She looked professional and comfortable all at the same time.

"You okay, Harvey?" she asked as she sat down next to me. "You're kind of staring."

I blushed and tore my eyes from her shoes. "Sorry. I was just admiring your shoes." I groaned. "That sounds awful given that Sidney is dead."

She put her hand on mine. "Thanks. And it doesn't sound awful. It sounds like coping. I've been pondering the slice of lemon meringue pie I brought for lunch. We all have to distract ourselves whatever way we can."

I squeezed her fingers and smiled. "Thanks. You okay?"

She nodded. "I just don't understand why someone would want to hurt Sidney." She shook her head. "I mean he was kind of a jerk sometimes, but only about library fines. Otherwise, he kept to himself. He was happier that way, I think."

I thought I knew what she meant. I'd invited Sidney to the shop for author readings and events, but he'd always declined.

He was supportive and often set up displays in the library that related to what I was doing in the store so that his patrons could participate if their budgets or other things kept them from buying books at my shop. But I got the distinct impression that groups of people were not his favorite thing.

Stephen and the sheriff came back to meet us, and Mindy and I both stood. Tuck and I had become good friends, and I was always glad to see him, even under these circumstances. But I knew this was going to be a hard day for him because he always took murder cases very seriously, especially since we seemed to have far more than our fair share of them in our tiny town. I knew Tuck would never say this, but it was also an election year. So if he wanted to keep his job, he had to be on the top of his game for everything, especially a murder.

"Show me, Harvey," he said with a nod.

I stood and smiled down at Mindy and was glad when Stephen sat down beside her. She seemed like she was handling things really well, but I knew that might just be a façade or that the reality might hit her out of the blue. It was good she not be alone.

I led Tuck back through the stacks to where Walter stood like he was part of a military parade. He had apparently taken his role very seriously.

"Thanks, Walter," Tuck said. "If you could wait with Stephen and Mindy after Deputy Watson clears the library. I'll need your statements."

Walter nodded and moved back across the library.

Tuck bent down, looked at Sidney, checked his pulse once again, and then sighed heavily. "Oh, Sidney." When he stood, he ran his hand over his shaved head and said, "He was just like this when you found him?"

I nodded. "I only touched him enough to check his pulse. But he wouldn't be under the table..."

"No, someone put him under there." He looked up at the ceiling and let out a long breath. "The coroner is on his way."

I studied my friend for a few moments while he took notes on the room. He had circles under his eyes, and his dark brown skin, which usually glowed because of his meticulous regimen of sunscreen and moisturizer, looked a little gray. He was tired, very tired. I told myself that I needed to stop and see him and his wife, Lu, later today, just to see how they were doing.

When Tuck finished his preliminary examination of the scene, we headed back up to the front desk where Mindy, Walter, Stephen, Lucy, and Deputy Watson waited. Tuck asked Lucy to come with him, and Watson interviewed me in the children's section. Then, they did the same "separate and question" routine with Stephen, Walter, and Mindy.

Given the look of frustration on Tuck's face after he finished his interviews, it seemed like none of us had told him anything useful. Whoever had killed Sidney had been quite stealthy. Somehow, that made his murder seem all the more unnerving, a feeling that got much stronger when Tuck and Watson began a careful search of the building to see if the killer might still be hiding inside.

When they had walked away, Walter said, "Don't you think the killer would have slipped out when Watson cleared the library earlier."

"I was just thinking the same thing," Mindy said. "That's what I would have done." She blushed. "Not that I did—"

I put my hand on her arm. "I know just what you mean. No one suspects you." I meant what I said, even though I knew it technically wasn't true. Anyone in the library, including Walter, Stephen, and me, was a suspect.

"Watson took everyone's names and numbers as he escorted them out of the library," Stephen said. "Maybe they figured that would be enough."

"Couldn't someone have just given false information?" I asked.

"If so, that would tell the police something wouldn't it?" Mindy suggested. "Although, how would the police find them if they gave false information?"

We all stood and stared at our hands for a minute as if we were too shy to note that our police department, our friends, might have made a really serious mistake.

I was just about to suggest that we didn't understand the ins and outs of police work when I saw a white man in a long coat run down the hallway toward the front door with Tuck right behind him. I rushed over to see what was going on and looked down the hall just in time to see the man punch the other police deputy who was guarding the door and dash off into the tree line with Tuck right behind him and Watson coming soon after.

"Maybe they don't need the contact information for the killer after all. Looks like they just need to catch him," Stephen said.

I sighed. The day had just gotten far more complicated.

2

Unfortunately, despite how fit and fleet of foot our police officers were, the man in the long coat eluded them, and when they came back to the library, they were winded and angry, both of them. "How did he do that?" Officer Watson asked as he bent over his knees to get his air back.

"He must know the town because we lost him down an alley," Tuck said as he looked at me. "Near your shop, actually."

I groaned. Of course the man had disappeared near my shop. Of course he had. "I'll keep an eye out," I said, trying to keep the weariness out of my voice given how tired Tuck looked. "Did you recognize him?"

"Oh yes, that was Joe Cagle. He works at the gas station at the edge of town. I'm sure you've seen him," Watson said as he stood and smoothed his long, blond hair back from his face. "Fine enough guy. But a little brusque, I guess."

"Fine enough until he ran from you," Walter snapped.

"Well, yes, that is suspicious," Tuck said with a knowing nod. "But Joe doesn't have a lot of extra cash. He's always picking up odd jobs to help make ends meet. He won't be able to stay away from his job long . . . unless he really has something to hide."

Mindy sat back down at the table. "We'll need to keep the library closed?"

Tuck nodded. "For a couple of days at least. We'll let people keep the idea that it was a water leak for as long as we can, though."

A bell rang from behind the counter. "That'll be the front door," Mindy said as she pushed herself to standing again.

"I'll go with you," Stephen said, "Just in case."

I looked at Tuck and then Deputy Watson, thinking one of them might want to be the "just in case" person on duty, but Tuck shook his head. "If we're looking to keep up the façade of a water leak, it's not going to work to have one of us answer the door." He pointed to his uniform.

"Ah, yes." I leaned against the table. "So this Joe Cagle guy? You think he might have killed Sidney?"

Tuck ran his hand over his head again. "I wouldn't have thought so, but people don't usually run unless they have something to hide."

Just then, the coroner and his assistant came in with a stretcher. "Point the way, Sheriff," he said.

Tuck led them back to Sidney's body, and within minutes, they had studied the scene and gotten Sidney up onto the stretcher. "Is there a back door we could use?" Tuck asked.

Mindy walked toward the back of the children's section with her keys in hand. "I just have to disable the alarm."

"We parked back here just to keep a lower profile, but I suspect we were noticed when we pulled in," the coroner's assistant said.

"Oh no doubt about it," I added as I looked at the text message on my screen. My dear friend Cate's message said, "Coroner at the library." I held the phone up for Tuck to see and then showed it to Mindy.

"Sorry," Tuck said as he and Mindy followed the stretcher. "I'll release a statement. Try to keep people away from here for a bit."

Mindy's shoulders sagged. A sad day had just gotten harder for her.

As soon as Sidney's body was loaded, Mindy re-locked and alarmed the back door. Tuck and Watson gave one more look around the area where Sidney's body had been and then they headed out, too. Then Mindy sent Lucy home with instructions to watch something fun and have some hot tea. Lucy smiled and left quietly.

"She'll be okay?" Walter asked. "I could drive her home."

"She'll be okay. Lucy lives at home with her mom and only works here because she's fresh out of school and hasn't found a teaching job yet. I'll let her mom know she's on her way." Mindy took out her phone and began to text.

"Can we help you tidy up and close the library?" I asked as she typed.

She looked up and smiled before nodding. "That would be nice."

Walter, Stephen, and I all headed in different directions to put unshelved books on the trolleys and straighten the sale tables. No reason Mindy needed to come back to a mess when she was able to reopen.

Whether I was driven by my morbid curiosity or random luck, I can't say, but I found myself back where Sidney's body had been. I tried to avoid the exact spot where I'd found him and straightened up the tables on the other side. That's when I saw it, a piece of paper sticking out from under one of the books.

I reached into the pocket of my sweater and took out the gloves I always carried along since the wind this time of year could be cold coming off the water. After putting one on my right hand, I tugged the paper out. It was the size of a small notepad, maybe three by five inches, and someone had scribbled, "Stiff, Roach, inside back cover."

I stared for a minute and then realized that the note referred to Mary Roach's book about cadavers, *Stiff*. It was one of my favorites by the author. Out of instinct, I did a quick scan of the tables, but I didn't see a copy of the book amongst the sale books. I moved over to the shelves and looked for the book there, but the space where it normally would have been shelved was empty.

My own investigative skills at an end, I carried the note carefully up to the front with a small stack of books to be shelved under my arm. "Do you have a bag?" I asked Mindy as we reconvened at the counter. "I think I found something."

She took a look at the note and said, "Oh, that's from Sidney's desk and it's his handwriting, too. He must have been looking for something for someone." She reached under the counter and pulled out a plastic sleeve like the ones that go around the CDs in audio books.

I slid the paper in. "Perfect. I need to get this to Tuck."

She nodded and picked up her keys again after giving the library one more glance. "Thanks. It looks good. Now, let's get out of here."

Stephen and Walter followed us out the doors to the hallway, which Mindy locked up behind us, and then we all walked out, our arms full of books, into the mid-day sun. The warm light belied the dark shadow that seemed to linger over all of us.

"You okay to get home?" I asked Mindy. "You can walk with me to my house, and I can drive you from there if you want."

"Nope, we've got her," Stephen said as he slipped an arm through Mindy's. "I'll ride with you, or drive your car if you prefer."

Mindy smiled. "That's not necessary." She wanted to sound certain, I could tell, but she definitely didn't.

"Our pleasure," Walter added. "I'll follow along like the chase car. Pretend you're in the Tour De France." He chuckled. "You okay, Harvey?"

"Totally fine," I said. "Texting Mart now." I held up my phone and wrote my best friend. "Found body at library. Going to the store. You free?"

"Be there with the dogs in ten," she replied.

Normally, I tried to stay away from my shop on the days I was off because I needed the space but also because I wanted my assistant manager, Marcus, to know I was confident in him. But today, I needed the comfort of my own store, even more than my home, because I wanted to be around people. I hoped Marcus would understand.

As I walked the couple of blocks to the store, I found myself scanning for Joe Cagle. I both hoped I would and prayed I would not see him. My phone was at the ready, but if he was dangerous, I could only hope that being out where other people were walking their dogs and taking a stroll in the warming spring air would keep me safe.

He was nowhere to be seen, though, and when I reached the store, I felt more relief than I'd expected and realized just how nervous I'd been. I opened the door and stepped through and heard the bell sound overhead. When Marcus looked up from the counter where he was ringing up a customer, I smiled in apology, but he gave me a look of complete understanding.

When Rocky, the café manager and Marcus's girlfriend, came over with a huge vanilla latte, I said, "You already heard?"

"Cate texted. She and Lucas are on their way. Lu's bringing us all lunch." She handed me the mug. "Word travels fast."

I sighed. "It sure does. Guess I better get in touch with Mom and Dad and Stephen and Walter, too."

"Already done," Marcus said from behind me. "I used the

group text to let everyone know we were gathering here. Pickle and Bear are on their way. Woody and Elle, too."

I smiled. "I hope Lu is bringing enough food."

"I think she's got it covered," Rocky said with a smile as she looked out the front window. There was Lu's food truck. She was parking right in front of the store.

"I'll say." Suddenly, I realized the bowl of cream of wheat with raisins that I'd had for breakfast was long gone, and I was famished. "Am I terribly rude if I don't wait?"

"Nope," Marcus said, "not as long as you cover the counter when you get back so I can get our order." He smiled at Rocky.

"You know I want some of that mole," she said with a smile before heading back to the café counter.

I stepped outside and took a minute to actually enjoy the spring day. The planter boxes in front of the shop were bursting with tulips that my friend Elle had planted last fall. They were all shades of red and purple, and the simple joy of them seemed to shake a bit of the darkness off of me.

By the time I was done basking and admiring, Lu had the window of her truck open, and I rushed over, eager to get in line before anyone else so that I could relieve Marcus for a few minutes. And so that I could get my tacos. "Hey Lu," I said as I looked up at my friend. "You okay?"

She sighed. "I'm fine. Glad to be here." She paused. "How was Tuck?"

"He looks tired. Is he okay?"

"He's okay, but election year is always hard. He has to fight twice as hard as anyone else just to keep his job." She winced. "They say racism is dead."

I groaned. "I really wish it was." Tuck was a black man in the South, and despite the wonderful job he did as sheriff, some folks here in this part of the Eastern Shore didn't like the idea of an African American sheriff. I'd known that, but I hadn't thought much about how that kind of prejudice might make winning an election hard. "People already campaigning against him."

Lu nodded. "Not so much against him, but more with the racist stuff about crime rates and black men."

"Despicable," I said. I wanted to say more, but I was at a loss. I'd just have to spend the next few months working hard to secure Tuck's win,. I could do that.

"But anyway, we have another murder, I hear." Lu shook her head. "That poor man."

"Yeah." I didn't know what else I could say. Tuck shared a lot with his wife, but it was his decision how much of an investigation he shared, not mine. "Thanks for coming out today. Could I get two chicken tacos with mole, please?" Lu made the best mole sauce I'd ever had, and I ate as much of it as I could.

"You got it. Figured you all might be my best customers today. Plus, I wanted to be with my friends." She gave me a wan smile and then served my food.

I could hardly wait until I got to the front counter to eat, but I resisted temptation and made it to the register before I took a bite. Marcus darted right out for his and Rocky's orders, and I scarfed down a whole taco as I watched a customer wend her way to the counter.

When she arrived, I finished chewing and apologized. "Sorry. Lunch on the go today."

She smiled and pointed to a corner of her mouth,. "You've got a little... "

I picked up a napkin and blushed. "Thanks. If you're hungry, I have to say that Lu makes the best mole in the world." I pointed toward the front of the store and the truck outside. "Great prices, too."

"Oh, that does sound good. Mind if I eat and read on your bench outside? It's just a lovely day," she asked as I rang up her books, which included a copy of *The Cracked Spine*, Paige Shelton's wonderful cozy mystery set in Edinburgh.

"I'd be disappointed if you didn't," I said sincerely. "Enjoy." I handed her the bag and smiled. But as soon as she was a few steps away, I dove into my second taco. I was sure Lu's food was good cold, but I didn't want to test the theory today.

As I finished, my best friend and roommate, Mart, arrived with my dogs, Mayhem and Taco. Most days I would have taken them for a walk with me, but this morning, I'd just felt like wandering without the worry of bathroom stops and tangled leashes. I was glad I'd made that call because it would have been a long morning of waiting outside the library if I'd taken them along.

Mart released them, and both pups bounded over. Well, Mayhem, a hound dog, bounded; Taco, the Basset, sort of lumbered. Their affection was similar – all squeals and wiggling butts – and I gave them each a good rub before sending them off to bask in the sunlight on their dog beds in the front window. They gladly obliged after a lap at their water bowl by the counter. Between their cuteness and the food truck outside, we might just have a high sales afternoon.

"You doing alright?" Mart said. "Hard morning?"

"Hard for sure, but yeah, I'm okay. Sadly, I guess I'm getting used to this whole 'find a body' thing." I sighed and slumped against the stool behind me. "Still, Sidney didn't deserve that."

"So it was the librarian, then? I'd heard a rumor, but you know how rumors are." She leaned her elbows on the counter. "Was it awful?"

I thought for a minute. "Well, yes, because he was dead." I stared at my friend with pretend disgust, but I knew what she really meant. "But no, he honestly looked like he was sleeping."

"Maybe he went peacefully?" She took a deep breath and looked out the front window. "I better get out there. The line is already getting long."

I followed her gaze and saw that, sure enough, Lu had ten or so customers waiting, including our friends Lucas and Cate.

They waved when I caught their eye and pantomimed to ask if I wanted anything. I held up my empty red and white paper bowl to show I'd already eaten, and they laughed.

Within minutes, all our friends were gathered in the café with Lu's food, and while normally we discouraged outside food, today it felt just fine to have this deliciousness in our space, Rocky and I agreed. When a few customers followed suit, I smiled and waved them on in. "Enjoy," I said because sometimes gracious hospitality is the antidote to very hard things.

We all huddled up around a bunch of tables pulled together, and Marcus and I took turns getting up to help customers. We talked about the weather and what everyone was doing for the rest of the weekend, and when Tuck arrived, we did our best to not talk about Sidney's murder. But our best didn't last long because Tuck needed to talk.

"It's just so sad. He really only wanted to be left alone to do his job and read. And he was set to retire in a couple of years." Tuck shook his head. "He just told me that last week when I stopped in."

"Oh, that is sad," Elle said. "Who wants to kill a reclusive librarian anyway?"

I sighed. "It doesn't make much sense at all." I sat back and looked over the store, letting my eyes naturally scan over the shelves. When they reached the creative nonfiction section, I sat up. "Oh, Tuck, I forgot to give you something."

I raced over to the counter and took my sweater off the stool to get the note in the CD sleeve. "I found this near where Sidney's body was. I don't know if it's relevant, but Mindy said that was Sidney's notepaper and handwriting." I handed him the sleeve.

He studied it for a minute. "You have any sense of what it means?"

I nodded. "It's a book. One sec." I went over to the shelf that my eyes had snagged on a few moments before and brought a copy of *Stiff* over. "This one."

Tuck took the book from my hands and flipped it over to read the back cover. "It's about what happens to dead bodies?"

I nodded. "It's fascinating," I said with enthusiasm. When I saw my friends' faces, I added, "It sounds bad, but it's actually a really fascinating and well-written book." I wasn't making headway here, so I stopped trying to explain and thought about how Roach herself must get similar looks all the time.

"Mind if I borrow this? I can buy it if you'd like," Tuck said.

"Nope, keep it. I'll get another." I smiled and said, "When will you know cause of death?"

Tuck sighed again. "Probably this afternoon."

I nodded and then asked the question I always had, "Anything we can do to help?"

Cate sat forward. "We'll bring you all dinner tonight, okay?" Lucas and Cate were both excellent cooks, and their gift to most situations was the perfect comfort food, including Lucas's amazing cupcakes.

Tuck smiled. "That would be great. Thanks. And Lucas, could I buy a dozen cupcakes for the station tomorrow? It's going to be long days for a bit, and the team could use a little pick-me-up."

"No, you may not," Lucas said sternly and then smiled. "I will give them to the department after I bake up a new batch tonight." He stood. "Thanks for lunch, everyone. Work calls." Lucas was the director at the local maritime museum.

"See you later, love," Cate said as she stood and stretched to kiss him on the cheek.

The rest of us also stood and moved the tables back while Elle and my mom cleared up our trash. "Lu's food always makes things better," Mom said as she patted me on the back. "Thanks for inviting us to join you."

My parents had moved to St. Marin's last summer, and

they'd quickly become an integral part of the circle of people I spent time with, which is not something I could have foreseen or would have even wanted a couple of years ago. Now, I didn't want to go a day without seeing them.

She and Dad lingered while everyone said their goodbyes and headed back to their workplaces and homes, but when Tuck asked to speak to me, Mom and Dad wandered into the bookstore so we could have privacy.

"I need to find Joe Cagle, Harvey. He didn't come into work as was expected, so now it's imperative I locate him." He studied my face. "I didn't want to announce that with so many people around," he said in a quieter voice, "but could you let everyone know to let me know if they see him?"

I'd long ago grown used to the way that our sheriff relied on his trusted friends for help with investigations. He simply had to, given how small his budget and, therefore, his staff, was. But he never breeched confidences or put his investigations in peril. He simply relied on us to be his "eyes and ears on the ground," as they said in those police shows.

"Absolutely. I'll send the text out right now. They should call your cell?"

"Perfect." I knew that some people might frown on the sheriff's methods, so I never questioned his requests, especially when it meant he kept his nose – and his phone – clean. No need to give his election any more trouble.

"Keep an eye out from Joe Cagle from the gas station. Call Tuck's cell if you see him. Related to this morning. Thanks." I kept the message short and sweet, and my friends responded with simple thumbs ups on the message. If Joe was in town, one of us would see him soon.

Mayhem and Taco had barely lifted their heads for the last hour, so I figured they'd be good for a bit longer. "Mind if those two stay with you for a bit?" I asked Marcus as I walked across the store to meet Mom and Dad.

"Well, they are a lot of trouble," Marcus quipped with a smile.

I laughed. "Thanks," I said and turned to my parents. "Fancy a walk by the water?"

"Sounds like a lovely idea," Dad said as he took his two women by the arm and led us to the door. "Treat you to ice cream?"

I grinned. "Now you're talking."

We strolled down Main Street past Elle's farm store and the art co-op that Cate managed. The police station looked quiet as we passed, and I hoped Tuck got a lead soon. That note was something, but it didn't tell him much without context.

We turned down the street that led to the maritime museum and made our way over to the shack where two teenage girls were serving ice cream to tourists. Dad ordered each of us a double cone, mine with mint chocolate chip and pralines and cream, and then we settled at a picnic table by the waterfront. Near us, the shipbuilders who worked for the museum were hard at work constructing a schooner, their latest project for the shipbuilding school they ran. So far, they had the hull built, and I could see some massive tree trunks to the side that I thought might become the masts. One of these days I was going to learn to sail . . . when I had the time.

Mom looked around and then said, quietly, "So why the guy from the gas station?"

I told them about Cagle running from the library and disappearing this morning, and Dad said, "That really surprises me. He seems like a straight-shooter, sort of a loner, too. Can't imagine he'd have any beef with a librarian."

I sighed. "Sidney was kind of a hermit in his own way. Maybe there was a recluse rivalry?" I smiled at my sorry attempt at humor, but then grew quiet. Two quiet men, both in the library. That wasn't surprising, but maybe there was something to that.

I was just beginning to let my mind follow that train of thought when movement near the water caught my eye, and I turned just in time to see Lucy, the children's librarian, drop something into the water. "What she's doing?" I said more to myself than my parents.

At first, I thought maybe it was bread for the birds or a rock or something, but when she saw me watching, she let out a little squeak and walked away quickly.

I stood and ran to the railing over the water just in time to see what looked like a bag sink below the surface.

3

With a look back at Mom and the fleeting back of Dad, who had taken after Lucy, I took out my phone and called Tuck's cell. As soon as I told him what had happened and that Dad had followed her, I heard his car door close. "Be there in one minute."

Mom and I moved closer to the parking lot so we could point Tuck in the right direction, and then Watson followed me over to the railing so that I could show him where the bag had sunk. I knew that information was mostly irrelevant given currents and such, but at least they'd have a place to start if they wanted to try.

Mom and I spent an anxious few minutes waiting for Dad and Tuck to return, but when they did, together, their faces were grim. "She slipped into a house, and I didn't feel comfortable following," Dad said.

"You made the right call, Mr. Beckett." Tuck looked over at Mom and me. "I went in, but she must have slipped out the back. It wasn't even her house. The poor woman who lived there was a good sport, though, said it was the most excitement she'd had in a long time." A small smile played over Tuck's mouth.

"I bet. A random girl in your house with the police coming after. She'll be talking about that for weeks," Mom said. "I would be."

We all stood gathered, the five of us, near the place where Lucy had thrown whatever it was she'd thrown, and I kept looking over at the water, hoping by some miracle that the bag would float to the surface again. It didn't.

"Are you going to send down a diver to look?" I asked.

Tuck and Watson exchanged a glance, and Tuck said, "Oh yes, we'll get out our elite SEAL team that works in conjunction with the police force to find a sandwich bag with stale crust in it."

I winced. I knew Tuck was teasing, and I knew he was under a lot of stress. But surely he didn't think I would make such a big deal out of littering, much as I hated it.

Tuck pulled a hand down over his face and looked at me. "Sorry, Harvey. I didn't intend that to sound so mean. It's just that we don't have divers available except for search and rescue, and since we don't know what was in—"

I put up a hand. "I understand. It's just that she really got scared when she saw me." I watched Dad as he strolled along the railing, looking just as I had been. "She was hiding something in there."

"I agree. But she did a good job of hiding it because I just don't think we can go after it." Tuck shook his head. "Sorry, Harvey."

I put my hand on his arm. "It's okay, Tuck. But are you okay?" I glanced over at Watson and saw his face mirror my own concern.

Before Tuck had a chance to answer, I heard Dad's voice from down on one of the piers where canoers and kayakers put in. "Can you grab that?" he called.

I wandered over to see what Dad was doing, and I saw a woman in a yellow kayak reaching for something beside her boat. When she lifted her arm, she had a small plastic bag in her hand.

She paddled over and gave it to Dad, who held it up to show me clearly. "This it?" he asked.

"Yes," I shouted and turned to wave Tuck, Mom, and Watson over only to realize they were right behind me. "Oh, wow. Here you are. Look!"

I pointed over at Dad, who was climbing the small set of stairs back up to us.

"We see, Harvey," Mom said with a smile. "Way to go, Burt."

Dad handed the bag to Tuck, who had already put on gloves. He slowly opened the bag, and I let out a collective sigh that Lucy had at least sealed the bag completely, which left the piece of paper inside completely intact.

When he unfolded it, he read, "Don't tell anyone, Sugar. You know what will happen. – Me."

Mom batted her eyes a few times, "Well, if that isn't a bit of manipulation, I don't know what is."

Watson put out his hand to Tuck, and the sheriff set the paper in it carefully. The deputy studied the paper by holding it up to the light, where it became clear the small sheet was a light pink, not white as it had seemed out of the sunshine. "Good quality note paper, Sheriff. Maybe twenty-eight pounds, not the cheap stuff."

I stared at Watson for a minute before I said, "You can tell a paper's weight by holding it?"

Watson grinned. "My parents run a copy shop down Easton. I grew up being able to tell a paper's weight and value by touch." He winked at me. "Don't get me started on ink."

"Actually," Tuck said, "Can you tell anything about the ink?"

Watson looked back at the sheet in his hands. "Looks like a standard ball-point pen to me." He turned the page over. "See how the writer pushed harder to write. It shows on the back, but that could also be because the person was upset."

Tuck nodded. "Alright, then, well, this is something, and it tells us a bit more about what happened with Sidney."

"You think someone was blackmailing him?" Dad asked.

I shook my head before Tuck could even answer, but when he looked at me, he said, "Yeah, I don't think so either, Harvey. I think someone wanted Sidney to recover this note for them."

I quickly explained the other note I'd found to Mom and Dad and told them how the book Sidney had been looking for went missing.

"So then, do you think it was the person who was doing the blackmailing that killed Sidney or the one who was being blackmailed?" Mom asked.

"That is a good question, Mrs. Beckett. One I aim to answer."

Tuck and Watson headed back to the sheriff's office, and given that our ice cream was long gone and our quiet afternoon no longer so quiet, Dad, Mom, and I walked back to the shop. The store was buzzing with activity, people reading and sipping coffee, and Marcus was handling recommendations and running the register with aplomb.

Still, given the crowd and my own need for distraction, I decided to stay. Mart was running a wine tasting over in Princess Anne, and she wouldn't be home until later this evening. I didn't feel like being alone, even with the dogs, so working for a few hours felt good.

I explained my rationale to Marcus because I didn't want him to think I considered him incapable, and he gave me a quick hug. "Oh, no, I'm glad for your help." He looked over at a young woman in her twenties. Her blonde hair hung straight to her chin, and her makeup was so expertly applied that it looked like she wasn't wearing any. "She wants books by women and about women's lives. 'Honest but not morose,' she said. When I offered to help, she said she'd just browse."

"Ah. I see," I fluffed my slightly wild curly hair. "I'm on it." I smiled at Marcus, who could easily have recommended a dozen books for her but still dealt with stereotypes and prejudice since he was a young, black man.

By the time I was done making my suggestions, the woman had a stack of books under her arm and had asked me to special order a copy of *The Midnight Library* on my assertion that despite the fact that it was written by a man, it was still a stellar work of women's fiction. Marcus rang up her purchases and weighed in on his feelings about her choices, affirming that he had learned a lot about the women in them from each title. When the woman left, she thanked us both, and I felt confident she'd be back and feel more comfortable taking Marcus's suggestions the next time.

The last hour of the day sped by with customers and a good bookish conversation with Marcus about the latest Rebecca Roanhorse book, *Black Sun*, and whether we liked books that ended with cliff-hangers like that one. By the time it was five, I felt more relaxed and ready to enjoy a quiet evening than I had a couple hours earlier.

I left Marcus to close up for the night and took Mayhem and Taco for a leisurely walk on the way home. The dogwoods were just beginning to flower, and the redbuds were a little past their prime. But still, the gentle whites and pinks of the trees combined with the bright blooms on the azaleas in people's yards spoke of the riot of color that would soon come to our temperate climate.

Once we got home, I let the dogs loose to run around the fenced backyard, and I did a little bit of weeding around the new peony bed I'd put in last year. The shoots of the shrubs were climbing high, and I could see a few buds already appearing. I was so eager for these hot pink flowers that I could hardly wait to see them and then display them in my kitchen. Hot pink was not a color I would have thought I'd love so much even a few years ago, but something about being well-established in middle age made me crave more color.

I peeked over the fence to find the dogs snoozing in the last remaining rays of sunshine and decided to let them be. Aslan, my cat, would appreciate a little of my undivided attention, even if she pretended she didn't.

Inside, I hung up my bag, slipped off my Birkenstocks, and plopped onto the couch. Aslan mewed with disdain but then sidled over and nestled against me. She was getting more and more plump in her old age, and while the vet kept insisting I put her on a diet, I hadn't yet decided to go that route, mostly because she could still do all she wanted, only ate twice a day, and deserved a little pampering since she lived with two very needy dogs.

I propped up my feet and studied my socks. The faces of multi-colored cats wearing glasses stared up at me, and I smiled. I wasn't as adventurous in my wardrobe as I was in my flower choices, at least not yet, but I had always appreciated whimsical socks.

With my head back against the sofa and Aslan purring away at my hip, I thought back over the wild events of my day off. I hadn't known Sidney particularly well, and the few times I'd brought a book back late, he'd scoffed and tried to shame me about responsibility. He did not take kindly to my assertion that I was simply trying to fund a new wing of the library. But still, he seemed like a good man, and his choice in acquisitions for the library was stellar. He stayed on top of the bestsellers in all the hot genres, but he also had a real dedication to featuring books by marginalized authors. His display for Pride month last June had been amazing with rainbow flags and titles by LGBTQ+ authors. When a few community members had pushed back about the display, he had simply said that the library was a public institution charged with representing and serving *all* of its patrons. I admired him for that.

The next thing I knew, a persistent scratching at the back door woke me up, and I realized that both Aslan and I had caught a quick cat nap. As I stood to let the dogs in, my stomach rumbled, and I looked at the clock on the stove. It was almost seven-thirty. I had slept for well over an hour. The events of the day must have caught up with me.

I texted Mart to see if she'd had dinner, and when she said she was surviving on the crackers they distributed to help the wine tasters cleanse their palates, I told her I'd have a meal when she got home. While the dogs snoozed, again, and Aslan watched from the top of the refrigerator, I pulled out the makings for my go-to tortilla casserole. I always kept the ingredients – instant corn muffin mix, a few cans of beans, a can of corn, cheddar cheese, and lots of spices – on-hand so that I could make an easy, hot meal quickly.

Within minutes, I had the casserole dish in the oven and was enjoying a glass of chardonnay while I delved into my latest read, *The Library of Lost And Found*. I was deep into the story and eager to learn about the secrets of Martha's family when the oven timer went off at almost the same moment Mart walked in the door. "Well, you couldn't have made a more fitting entrance," I said as I lifted the warm casserole and put it on top of the stove.

"That smells amazing," she said and looked at my empty wine glass, "and I need to catch up."

I laughed. "Like you haven't been tasting at work."

"Okay, maybe a little." She tucked a loose strand of her dark hair behind her ear, and I, not for the first time, admired my best friend's fair and flawless complexion. The smattering of freckles around her nose and cheeks set off her porcelain skin, and while I knew she didn't like her freckles, I adored them.

She reminded me of Pippi Longstocking, or maybe of Pippi and Snow White's child. "Your day get any better?"

"Ha," I spat. "Depends on what you mean by better." I spent the next few minutes dishing our food and getting Mart caught up on the day's events, and by the time we sat down on the couch with our plates and our glasses, she was shaking her head.

"So let me see if I got this right. Sidney was looking for a book that contained a note from a blackmailer to the blackmailee when someone killed him?"

I nodded.

"But somehow, Lucy had the note and tried to dispose of it and ran when you caught her?"

I nodded again.

"Now, then, Tuck has two suspects, both of whom ran when it seemed like they might be caught doing something they shouldn't do."

"You got it," I said after I took a long sip of my wine. "It seems like Sidney just got caught up in something because someone accidentally donated a book with a note to the library."

"Gracious. Makes me want to be sure to shake out the pockets and open the covers of anything I might donate anywhere," Mart said with a slow shake of her head.

"Same here." I studied my book on the coffee table. "I guess the killer must have taken the copy of Roach's book with them."

Mart sighed. "Are you thinking that the book was important somehow? Beyond the note from inside it, I mean?"

I shrugged. "Maybe." Something niggled at the back of my mind, and I sat quietly to see if I would come to mind.

"How do you think Lucy got the note? Do you think she killed Sidney?"

The thought I'd been trying to drag out of the back of my

mind flashed forward. "She must know where the book is," I almost shouted as I sat forward.

"What?!" Mart asked.

"I mean if she had the note, then she probably had the book, too, right?" My mind was racing ahead.

"Maybe," Mart said with emphasis. "But couldn't the note have just fallen out and Lucy found it? Or if she killed Sidney, couldn't she have just taken the note out of the book and left the book there?"

I sat back. "I guess she could have just taken the note, but the book wasn't there. I looked." I tilted my head. "I looked on the sale tables and in nonfiction, but what if Lucy stashed the book somewhere else in the library?"

Mart sighed. "We're going to the library aren't we?"

I smiled. "Maybe Tuck will let us tag along to look."

"You never learn do you?" Mart groaned. "Okay, but not alone. Tomorrow, we can ask Tuck if we can both go with him."

Mart had good reason to be concerned. I'd gotten myself into a lot of jams in the past when my curiosity had gotten the better of me. "Sounds good. I'm texting him right now."

The sheriff replied almost immediately. "Good thought. I'll check it out tomorrow."

I wrote right back. "Mind if I come along. I mean I know what the book looks like."

"You gave me a copy, Harvey. I know what it looks like, too." There was a pause in his message, "But you can come. You might find it more quickly than I can."

Tuck humored me a lot more than most police officers would, and I was grateful. "Thanks. What time?"

"Nine? Then you can get to work."

"Perfect. Oh, and Mart is coming," I added.

He sent back a simple eyeroll emoji.

"We're in," I said with a grin.

"Great," Mart answered with her own eyeroll. "It's never dull with you around, Harvey."

"Would you want it any other way?" I asked as I grabbed the remote. "Ready for more of *The Order*? I have to know if vampires are going to be part of this deal. It's the only urban fantasy trope they haven't incorporated yet."

Mart laughed. As long as I get to see more of Randall, I'm in." Mart loved the goofy, loyal werewolf on the show, and I couldn't blame her. He was a delight, even if the bookish Hamish was more my speed.

4

The next morning, I woke early and decided to make Mart and me a stellar breakfast with my extra time. Fortunately, one of our silent agreements was that we always stocked the best breakfast food, so in no time, I had ground sausage on and had fired up the crepe maker Mart had splurged on a few weeks earlier. I figured I could do a savory crepe with eggs, sausage, and cheese. We'd have to eat it with a knife and fork instead of in a cone like the take-out crepe places did, but I figured it would still be delicious.

Soon, the kitchen was sizzling, and the smell was heavenly, especially when I brewed us a pot of coffee with vanilla and cinnamon, a trick I'd learned from Rocky. It didn't take long for Mart to wander out and smile. "That smells amazing," she whispered as she rubbed the sleep from her eyes.

"You have about five minutes if you want to just relax." Mart had done so much for me since we'd moved across country from San Francisco, and while I could never repay her for her kindness, I did try to show my appreciation in little ways. "I'll bring you a cup of coffee. Are you taking cream or not these days?"

My best friend had recently discovered she was lactose intolerant, but sometimes, she used her magic pills and still indulged. "No cream today," she said. "I'm saving my dairy for ice cream later."

I smiled. "That's my girl."

We spent the next half-hour enjoying our breakfast and watching the birds scatter as Taco leaped at them in the backyard while Mayhem lay in yet another sunbeam. It was a perfectly quiet morning, and I was grateful for it, especially given the day we'd had yesterday.

Soon, though, it was time to meet Tuck at the library, and despite the fact that Mart knew Tuck would be there, she insisted on going. She played her desire off like she was just looking out for me, but I guessed there was some curiosity on her part, too. Besides Mart was almost as much of a book lover as I was, so any chance to be around books was hard to pass up for either of us.

When we parked by the library's front door, Tuck and Mindy Washington were just unlocking things. I was a bit surprised to see Mindy, but given that she had the keys, it made sense she was there.

Greetings exchanged, Tuck explained to Mindy that we were looking for something and then said, "Maybe you'd like to catch up on email or something while we look? We can let you know what we find." He phrased the suggestion like a question, but it wasn't really one.

Mindy frowned and said, "You don't want my help to look for, well, whatever it is you're looking for." She was fishing for information, and I couldn't blame her. I was actually a little surprised that Tuck hadn't explained our purpose.

Tuck shook his head. "I don't want anyone to cast aspersions on you, Mindy. If you aren't involved with anything about this case, I think it's better. Just know we're looking for a particular book."

She nodded and gave Tuck a small smile. "Well, thanks. I'll be in my office if you need me." She turned, lifted the counter to go behind the desk, and slipped into the glass-fronted office behind.

As the three of us moved off into the stacks, I quietly said to Tuck, "She's a suspect?" It was the only reason I could think of why Tuck would let Mart and me look for the book but not the librarian.

The sheriff gave me a small nod. "She is. Not a serious one, mind you. But still, I thought it better she not know exactly what we're doing."

Mart huffed. "You did tell her you'd share what we found." She raised one eyebrow.

"I did, but that doesn't mean I will tell her exactly." He shook his head. "I do know what I'm doing, you know?" He tried to sound like he was teasing, but that edge was back in his voice.

"Of course you do," Mart said quickly with a glance at me. "Of course. Now, how do we do this?"

Tuck showed Mart exactly what the book looked like, and I noticed he kept his body between Mindy's office and the book, so he really was keen on not letting her know what we were seeking.

Then he gave us our marching orders. He went back to the nonfiction section to double-check the tables and shelves there, and he sent Mart to the fiction stacks and me to the children's section. "We need to check everywhere."

I made my way over to the colorful area beside the library's back room and started to scan the picture book shelves. A trade paperback book would stand out amongst all the thin, tall books there, but I didn't see it. A scan over the middle-grade shelves didn't turn it up either, and when I carefully inspected the YA collection, it wasn't there either. I did one more pass over all the shelves, but it wasn't there.

Soon, I saw Mart headed back to where Tuck was still looking in nonfiction, and I joined them. "Nothing?" I said as the two of them looked up.

"Not a thing," Mart said. "You?" She looked from me to Tuck.

Both of us shook our heads. Tuck said, "Mart will you help me scan here one more time, and Harvey, would you let Mindy know we'll be ready to go in a minute?"

I nodded and headed toward the office, giving a look at the new release and best seller shelves as I went. Still nothing. I came at Mindy's office from the side, so I guess she didn't see me coming because when I went through the door, she squeaked and dropped something onto the floor.

I apologized for startling her and bent over to pick up what she'd dropped beside her desk. It was a copy of *Stiff*, and Mindy looked horrified that I'd seen it.

As I stepped to the door to call Tuck and Mart, I kept my eyes on Mindy. I didn't know what was going on here, but it didn't look good. Fortunately, Mindy didn't move, and Tuck and Mart came quickly. "She had the book," I said a little breathlessly as I held it out before me.

Tuck took the book from my hands and then turned to face Mindy. "What's going on here?"

She shrunk back in her black desk chair. "I didn't realize you all were looking for this title." She let out a long breath. "But I did know you were looking for a book, and I should have told you about the ones in here."

She looked at Tuck with a plea in her eyes. "This is where I say I was afraid it would make me look like I had something to do with Sidney's death and then you say that hiding it made me look more guilty. I'm sorry. I just didn't know what to do."

Tuck set the book down and put on gloves. "This may be useless at this point, but I still need to hold a pretense of decorum." He flipped over the cover and read the inscription aloud: "To my Sweet Sugar and all her morbid curiosities."

"Sweet Sugar?" Mart said. "Is that a girlfriend? A daughter? Boyfriend?"

"Where did you find this, Mindy?" Tuck said.

It wasn't lost on me that he was going along with her story, but I'd known Tuck long enough to know that he would go along with a lot if he thought it might find the killer.

"In the book return, actually. I thought someone had just accidentally put one of the sale books into the slot, so when I tidied up yesterday, I slid it onto my desk so I could return it to the sale when we opened." She raised her right hand. "I swear."

I glanced down to see if she also had a Bible on her desk, but I only saw a plastic wrapped copy of *The Bean Trees*, and I didn't think swearing on a book by Barbara Kingsolver made it any more likely she was telling the truth.

Tuck nodded but said, "It would have looked a lot less suspicious if you just told us you had the book when we first got here and heard we were looking for one." He gave Mindy a stern stare.

She nodded. "I know."

"Alright, well, we have it, at least we think we do, right?" He looked over at me. "This is the correct book?"

"It is. Do you have this book in the library collection?" I asked Mindy.

She shook her head. "That's how I knew it had been put in the drop by mistake. I looked it up yesterday."

"You didn't want it for your collection? Don't you scan the books people donate to see what the library can use?" Mart asked.

I almost answered this one for Mindy because I thought I knew what she'd say, but I was learning to talk less and listen more. So I did just that.

"Paperbacks don't last long around here. Too much wear and tear," she said simply.

Mart took a deep breath. "Makes sense," she said as she looked at the human body with a toe tag on the front cover. "Feels a little too on-the-nose to have a book about cadavers be related to a murder doesn't it?"

"I'm thinking that might not be a coincidence," I said before I thought to stop myself.

Everyone looked at me, but only Tuck spoke. "Why is that?

I shook my head. "I'm not sure. The book is about what happens to human bodies after we die, like when they're donated to science or body farms or whatever. But it's been a while since I read it, so I can't figure out what connection is teasing at the back of my brain."

"If you figure it out . . ." Tuck asked

"You'll be the first to know," I said with a quick glance at my phone. "I better get going, unless you need me here, Tuck."

"Nope, let's all clear out. We have what we need," Tuck said and let us all exit, including Mindy, before him. He stood nearby while she locked the office door and then as she locked the front doors behind us again.

"I won't leave town," Mindy said very seriously.

Tuck had his back to her, but I could see a small smile play at the corners of his mouth before he said, "Good. Stay close. We may need to bring you in."

Mindy's shoulders dropped and she headed off to her car as Mart and I turned toward mine. We had just started pulling out when Tuck came to my window. "Thanks for coming out, ladies."

"Anytime, Tuck," Mart said as she leaned over me.

"Yep, anytime. You don't think Mindy did this, do you?" I knew he'd say that he didn't rule out anyone at this point, but I was hoping he found her to be as sincere as I had.

"I doubt it, but you know that I don't rule—"

"Good," Mart said. "Now, go home and relax. You could use it."

Tuck frowned just a little but then waved as we drove away.

"He looks exhausted," Mart said as I turned onto the side street and headed toward the bookstore. "This case that draining you think?"

"I'm not sure. I think it's the election, but he does seem to be more on edge than usual." I made a note to ask Lu if I could do anything to help. Maybe there was a way we could support Tuck and lift a little of his burden.

I was only a few minutes later than usual in opening the bookshop, but Rocky already had the coffee brewing and the chairs off the tables. It smelled amazing inside.

With a quick wave and a smile in her direction, I got about my opening chores of turning on lights, unlocking the register, and doing a quick pass to straighten the shelves. This last task was always an exercise in ritual rather than necessity on the days I opened after Marcus closed because he always shelved every book before he left for the night. That was no small feat on a Saturday evening when browsers were plentiful. Still, I liked the routine of walking the shelves and visiting all the books before the customers came in.

With everything ready and Rocky set with a fresh, warm stash of her mother's cinnamon rolls, I opened the doors to find, to my delight, a young couple with an infant waiting to come in. They were friendly and pleasant, but they looked haggard. It was a look I recognized from many of my friends who'd had children over the years – sleep deprivation. While they walked quietly through the store as the baby slept, I asked Rocky for two lattes, one regular and one decaf, in case the baby was nursing, and two of those cinnamon rolls. Then, I met the couple near the fiction shelves, pointed to two armchairs and a footstool and put the drinks and rolls between them. "Sit. Rest. Enjoy. My treat. This one's decaf just in case," I whispered.

I saw tears well up in the eyes of the woman carrying the baby, and her partner smiled at me and said a quiet thank you after clearing her throat. I left them to have a still moment out in public while the baby slept on.

This kind of thing was one of the perks of owning my own business – I could give away whatever I wanted and only had to answer to me. Of course, in this case, I would pay Rocky for what I gave away because she was now the majority owner of the bookstore café, having decided to stay on for a while after graduation while she made some choices about her next career steps.

Sunday mornings were always quiet in the shop since a lot of people around here went to church, but I loved this morning most because there was an air of stillness that permeated the space. It reminded me of the years just after I graduated from college when I spent Sunday mornings on the floor of my apartment with the newspaper. I'd read and sip coffee and listen to the sounds of the city waking up around me.

Today, I helped a young man with an amazing mohawk find a book about World War II for his great-grandfather, and then a teenage girl in a long skirt came in and asked me to point her toward the sci-fi section. I walked over with her, shy as she was, and told her that *Ender's Game* was one of my favorite titles. When she saw there were four more books, she decided they would be her reading project for her English class. "My teacher is really cool. He wants us to find something we love and study it."

"Oh, he does sound amazing. Do you go to school here in St. Marin's?" I asked.

"Yep, his name is Mr. Evans. I'm going to suggest he come here." She met my eyes for the first time. "Is that okay?"

"Please do." I walked with her to the register and rang her up with the promise of a ten percent discount for anyone in Mr. Evans' class who mentioned him to me. She left smiling, and I grinned as I went to check on the young moms. They'd both fallen asleep, and the baby was still snoozing. If I'd had lap blankets, I would have covered them all up.

With everything quiet in the shop, I wandered the shelves again, considering what our next window display might be. I needed to do a summer reading collection of some sort, but the beach reads theme was a little tired, especially since we lived on the water. I thought about doing another local history display, but I'd done that before and decided we'd put that on a table instead. We needed something more catchy for the front window.

I stared out through the plate glass and tried to ignore the copious amounts of dog hair I needed to vacuum out of Mayhem and Taco's beds and looked at the trees that lined the street outside. That's when it came to me – I was going to do a tree display and ask Cate to make me a tree on which to set the books. She was always thrilled to do something "crafty," as she called it, and it would be a fun way for us to spend some time together.

As I headed back to the register to grab my phone and text her, I picked up a couple of titles including *Braiding Sweetgrass* by Robin Wall Kimmerer and *The Overstory* by Richard Powers. Wall's book wasn't strictly about trees, but it was a beautiful ode to the richness of nature and plants, and Powers books was one of the most amazing novels I'd ever read. I figured I could find some coffee table books that featured specimen trees, and I had a couple of field guides to trees, too. I was starting to get excited.

Cate readily agreed to help me out and suggested she had some time that afternoon if that might work. When she said she'd bring the supplies, I jumped on the chance. I wasn't someone with patience when it came to creativity. I wanted to do all the things at once, so this afternoon sounded perfect.

Besides, I kind of wanted to talk with Cate about Tuck. All morning, I'd been worried about him. He was a serious police officer, a good one who didn't make light of his job, but he was also a prankster and a kind of light-hearted guy. I hadn't seen any of that lightness in a while.

Since I had my phone out, I took the chance to message Lu and ask if she could stop by today.

"I just set up by the Baptist church. I have a few minutes before the rush begins. On my way." Her reply was quick, and once again, I admired her business acumen. The after-church flow of people was a very smart spot to put her food truck since that group often went out for a meal after services. I knew that Max's restaurant was always packed, and the Italian place at the edge of town, too. Even we got a pretty good run of folks who were looking for pastries for picnics or brunches when the services started ending.

I had just finished ringing up the purchases of the young moms with the infant – they'd bought a copy of Anne Lamott's *Operating Instructions* at my suggestion since it was a quite funny but honest look at motherhood – and accepting their gratitude for a place to rest and the snack when Lu came in.

She was dressed in her usual of scrubs and a brightly printed top, and today, her dark-brown hair was plaited into a strand that ran around her head. When she saw me at the counter, she smiled and jogged over. "Hola, Harvey."

"Hola, Lu. I won't keep you," I took her arm and turned us both away from the main store floor, "but I'm worried about Tuck. Is he okay?"

A shadow passed over Lu's face. "No."

I waited for her to say more, but when she didn't, I asked, "Is there anything I can do to help? Something he needs for the election maybe?"

Her eyes flicked up to mine, and her jaw relaxed a little. "You are a savvy one, Harvey Beckett."

I rolled my eyes. "So it's getting worse."

This time, she nodded. "It happens every time. As soon as

election year starts, these *perdedores* show up with threats and promises about how they're going to get a police officer instead of a criminal into office. It gets worse every day until the election is done."

"What in the world?!" I took a deep breath. "Can we address these idiots? Give them a piece of our minds."

She shook her head. "No. I'm afraid not. If we call these people out, Tucker looks defensive."

"And that just gives them fuel, right?" These people were despicable.

"Right. We just need to support him and help his campaign. Maybe you could put a sign for him in your window."

"Done." It felt like a tiny thing in the face of such hatred, but if it would help, even just to boost Tuck's morale, I'd hang twenty of them.

"You don't feel awkward about that?" Lu drew her eyebrows together. "A lot of the businesses don't like to take sides."

I rolled my eyes. "I run this business. I own this building. I can do whatever I want, and I, Harvey Beckett, owner of All Booked Up, endorse Tucker Mason for sheriff of St. Marin's." I even put my hand over my heart for emphasis.

The light came back into Lu's eyes. "I have some signs in the truck. If you get a minute, come get one?"

"Of course." I looked down at my phone. "You better go, though? Church is getting out."

Lu grinned and sprinted out the door and down the street. As I watched her run, I wondered what else I could do to support Tuck's campaign, and I felt ideas for an event start to spin in my head.

SOON, though, the after-church crowd descended in full force, and I was so busy recommending books and ringing up sales that I could only wave when Mart dropped off Taco and Mayhem on her way to an event at the winery.

By late afternoon, I was beat. Cate and I had gotten the tree display made and up, and it looked amazing. But we'd been busy all day, and I'd had to move back and forth between helping customers and helping Cate.

Now, though, the rush of customers had thinned, and I had a chance to sit back, prop my feet on the counter, and sip the decaf vanilla latte that Rocky had brought me. She'd sold out of cinnamon rolls early on, so I was glad she'd added to her baked goods in the past few weeks. Her pastry case was almost empty now, and I hoped that meant she'd had a good day financially. She deserved it.

I was just about to go over and pay Rocky for the lattes and cinnamon rolls I'd taken earlier in the day when Mindy Washington came in. As a true book lover, Mindy often shopped in my store despite having access to pretty much any book in the world through the library. "Some books you just need to own, you know?" she'd told me once, and I'd agreed.

Today, though, I suspected she wanted something more than the latest N.K. Jemisin book for her collection. "Hi Mindy. How are you?" I genuinely wanted to know because Mindy was a friend. But I also felt a little suspicious that she'd come in to my store a day after she'd been hiding evidence.

As soon as she saw me, she headed right over, and I took that as a good sign. At least she wasn't playing games or trying to act all sly or something.

"I've been better, Harvey, to be honest." She shrugged and refused to meet my eyes.

I noticed the dark circles under her eyes, and the kerchief around her usually perfectly-styled hair. "Yeah, I can imagine. Want to talk about it?" I looked around the shop, saw that everyone looked content for a minute, and pointed to the nearest café table.

"I'd like that. It's why I came in." She followed me to the table and dropped into the chair. "I needed to talk about what happened with someone, but . . ."

"But you couldn't because it's an active police investigation." I hoped that was the reason rather than that she didn't want to implicate herself.

"Exactly. I've already made Tuck's job hard enough. I didn't want to make things worse, especially with the election." She tugged her indigo kerchief down her forehead a bit.

"You've heard the talk?"

She sighed. "Of course. It's no surprise, but you'd think after serving three terms that people would just get it and back off." She squeezed her hands so tightly that they went from dark brown to near-white. "I feel just terrible about what happened yesterday."

She looked so forlorn that I couldn't help but reach over and put my hand on hers. "Want to tell me about it from the beginning?"

A long slow breath escaped her lips, and she smiled. "I would. Do you have time?"

I glanced around and caught Rocky's eye. She nodded and moved closer to the register in the bookshop. She was fully trained on my side of things, too, and since her café was empty, I knew she'd help out with sales for me if needed. I, again, felt deep gratitude for my amazing friends. "We've got a few minutes," I said, "and I'd like to understand."

Mindy nodded. "Like I said, I found the book in the drop on Friday. It was just in amidst all the other books, but I noticed it right away because it didn't have a label."

I thought of the couple of times I'd seen books from the library on my shelves, left there by people with fines, I expected, who wanted to return the book but felt embarrassed. I'd always spotted the books right away because of the white library label on the bottom of the spine.

"I had really just put it on my desk to deal with when we reopened, but when you all said you were looking for a book," she paused and took a deep breath, "I thought it might be the one you needed. I was going to turn it over, but first, I wanted to be sure it didn't implicate Sidney in something awful." I heard the catch in her throat and tightened my grip on her hands.

"You didn't think he'd be doing something unseemly, did you?" I wasn't sure where this was going, but I wanted to encourage Mindy forward into whatever she wanted to tell me.

"No, I didn't. Sidney was an odd guy, but also one of the kindest people I've ever known. If he was mixed up in something, it was because he was trying to help." She sighed. "He wasn't always the smartest when it came to judging character."

I'd often been accused of the same thing, so I got it. And her description of Sidney meshed with what I knew of the man.

"My mama would say he had the 'innocent as doves' part down, but needed to work on being 'wise as serpents.'" Mindy smiled again as she looked up at me. "It's a verse from the Bible about how to be a discerning person in the world."

I nodded. I liked that and wondered if Mindy's mama would say the same thing about me. "So you think it's possible he got involved with whatever happened because he was trying to help someone out?"

Mindy nodded. "I'm thinking he was trying to find that book for someone because they asked him to, and whatever was in there . . ."

It wasn't my place to tell Mindy about the note we'd found, but I did think it would be okay if I told her that Mart and I had come to the same conclusion. When I did, she sighed, and I saw her shoulders drop just a little in relief.

Still, I would be remiss if I didn't see what else Mindy might know about the book or the note. I just had to be careful how I asked. "Any idea who Sweet Sugar might be?"

Mindy raised her eyebrows and looked at me. "It's not

exactly the kind of name people use when checking out library books." She smiled.

"Good point. It feels very personal though, doesn't it?" I kept thinking it felt paternal, like a name for a daughter, but I wasn't sure.

"It does. But what were the 'morbid curiosities' the note mentioned?" She sighed. "I mean besides the book's content itself."

"I was wondering the same thing," I said. In my years on this earth, I'd met a lot of truly lovely people who had appreciation for things that absolutely creeped me out. One guy I knew was so fascinated with the Church Of Scientology and debunking them as a legitimate religion that he ran a social media-based Scientology month every April. I learned a lot from him, and he was a good friend. But I wasn't interested in going that deep into L. Ron Hubbard's life. "Maybe she was fascinated by death?"

Mindy shrugged. "Maybe." She stood up and stretched. "Thank you, Harvey. I feel better, which is selfish I know."

"Nope, not selfish. Believe me, I've been the focus on an investigation myself, and it's a heavy thing. Come talk anytime." I walked her to the door. "When can you reopen?"

"Tuck gave me the go-ahead for tomorrow, so we'll see how that goes." She opened the door to the street. "I figure it'll be either empty or slammed."

"Plan for slammed. St. Mariner's themselves have a pretty big fascination with death." I knew that morbid curiosity all too well.

5

I ran out of time and energy on Sunday evening, so when Lu dropped off Tuck's "Mason for Sheriff" sign I slipped it behind the counter for Monday morning. When I came in about Noon, as scheduled, Marcus had already done his magic with both the sign and a display around it. He'd hung Tuck's sign off to one side of the display, prominently but not absurdly so, and at the top of the window, he'd made a banner that said, "Good Cops/Bad Cops" with an arrow from "Good Cops" pointing down to Tuck's sign. It was lovely.

The books around the signs were perfect, too. He had displayed *The End of Policing* by Alex S. Vitale, *Mindhunter* by John E. Douglas, and Richard Scary's *A Day at the Police Station* among other titles that both supported police officers and critiqued them. It was a thoughtful display, one that didn't laud police officers as perfect or glamorize their tough jobs but that also brought up what I knew Marcus and I believed to be real needs for reform in policing, reforms that Tuck not only supported but had also started to implement in his position.

I knew we'd get some flak for some of the titles from the people who hung the "blue line" flags outside their houses, but honestly, I didn't care. Another perk of running my own business was that I could sell and display what I wanted, as long as I was ready for the blowback.

On the other side of the store, Marcus had picked up where I had left off the night before with my tree display. Cate had created a lovely, simple tree trunk and branches from some craft paper and a little paint, and then she'd hung photographs – her medium of choice – of tree leaves all around the branches. Then, I'd tucked book holders into the branches.

Now, Marcus had filled all those holders with the books I'd picked out and some more he'd found on our shelves including *The Hidden Life of Trees* by Peter Wohlleben and a couple of wonderfully illustrated picture books. The contrast between the two windows was stark – with the police display being sparse and largely monochromatic because of the covers and this one feeling sumptuous and lush with all the greenery. When I stepped outside, each window felt captivating in its own way, and I was sure we'd see an uptick in sales of these titles immediately.

It had apparently been quite a slow morning because not only had Marcus, with the help of Rocky, gotten the displays up, but he had also taken the time to make a list of the titles in each window as well as other related titles. Then, he'd made copies of those lists and placed them on a small table next to each display. Finally, he'd ordered at least one copy of every book on the list so that we'd have them the next day if someone asked for a particular book. It was a brilliant bit of marketing on his part, and I was grateful for all his work.

"Did you let Tuck know about what you've done?" I asked Marcus as he petted Taco behind his ears and made him groan.

"No, I thought you'd want to show him. It was your idea." My assistant manager was far too humble.

"Well, I'm going to tell him it was your idea because it was, and a brilliant one at that." I took out my phone and texted

Tuck to ask him to come by, and then I sent Lu a similar text, knowing she might be too slammed to come for a few hours. Lunch was always her busiest time.

But surprisingly, they both came in a few minutes later, arm in arm. Tuck was in jeans and a polo, and Lu had a flowered skirt. Clearly, neither of them was working today. "Good for you for taking a day off," I said as I hugged both of them at the same time.

"We needed a break, and Watson has things handled at the station."

I giggled a little. "Does he ever call you Sherlock?" I quipped.

Tuck rolled his eyes. "You are too bookish for your own good, Harvey." He grinned. "I left my pipe at home." He turned back to the front window. "That display is amazing, Harvey. Thank you."

"Don't thank me; thank Marcus. He did it." I pointed toward my assistant, who was helping an older man select a presidential biography. "I hope it's okay." I was suddenly a little nervous that we might have overstepped or made things difficult for Tuck.

Lu reached out and squeezed my arm. "It's more than okay. This is exactly the kind of platform that Tucker is running on, right?"

Tuck nodded. "You know I've been making some changes in how we do things here, and this display highlights that in just the right way. I couldn't critique other police officers, but between you and me, I think we need a major change in how we do things. This display captures that but doesn't have to come from me." He smiled again. "Thank you, sir."

Marcus stepped up from behind me. "You're welcome." The two men wandered over to the window as they talked about which titles Marcus had chosen and why.

"He seems a little better today," I said.

Lu nodded. "He is. It helps that he found Joe Cagle last night."

"Oh, wow. Great." I wanted to ask about four hundred questions, but I knew Lu wouldn't tell me anything. She was very cautious about sharing things about Tuck's work and for good reason. Too much chatter could really compromise an investigation. "I hope that what Cagle said was helpful."

"It was," she smiled and then moved me toward the café. "Now, let's get some coffee." It was clear that she and I would not be talking about Cagle any further just then.

We got our decaf drinks and sat down at the café table nearest the register, just in case Marcus needed me to ring someone up, and I enjoyed the companionable silence with my friends for a few minutes.

But then she said, "I was wondering if you wanted to help me with a fundraiser at the library."

The statement was so out of the blue that it took my brain a minute to catch up. "A library fundraiser? Are they short on money?"

She shrugged. "I have no idea, but I figure more books can't hurt, right?" She avoided eye contact with me, so I knew something was up. But I trusted my friend.

I nodded. "Right." Her points were solid. Every library could always use more funds, but this looked like more than just a general fundraiser. "But there's more, right?"

"Sidney was one of my best customers." Lu's eye were shining. "I want to do something to honor him. He was a good man."

"He was," I said. Every time someone said that to me, I wished I'd taken the time to get to know him better. "I'd be happy to help. What did you have in mind?"

"Oh good. I was hoping you'd say that because I already talked to your mom this morning." She grinned, and I sighed.

"Of course you did." And as if on cue, the bell over the shop door rang, and my mother walked in like she was entering a red carpet gala. Of course, my mother always walked that way. Her poise was impeccable, which is one of the many characteristics that made her a stellar fundraiser. She'd done this kind of work for years when my dad ran his company in Baltimore, and now that she was here in St. Marin's, she'd already made quite the reputation raising money for organizations big and small in the area.

Mom sat down and took my hand. "Luisa has told you her idea?"

Total Mom move there, to assume I'd said yes, but then she knew me and that I was always in for a good cause. "We were just getting to that," I said as I turned to Lu.

"I was thinking we could have a food truck fair in the library parking lot," Lu said with glee. My friend wasn't someone who exuded delight. She was usually warm-hearted but a little reserved. Today, though, I could almost her imagine her clapping her hands like a little child with a new toy might.

"Exactly. We'll do up the parking lot with lights and borrow some picnic tables. I thought the library could open their book sale up again, and we'd ask all the vendors to donate a portion of the proceeds," Mom added.

I could picture it, and it sounded lovely . . . and if I could picture it, Mom had already gotten all the details worked out in her mind. And I knew from experience that as simple as this sounded, my mother would want to go whole hog on the event.

"I think that sounds amazing. When are we thinking?" I braced myself because Mom did not do long timelines for these kind of things.

"Friday night," Lu almost shouted. She really was excited.

I took a deep breath. "We have four and half days to pull this off. Can we really do this? And isn't Friday night a big food truck night over in Annapolis?"

"That's the beauty," Mom said without even a second's hesitation. "Lu has already contacted ten trucks who usually sell over there on the waterfront, and they've agreed to come here." She stopped talking, and I could see big caveat coming.

"How many people do we have to guarantee we'll bring out?" I took a deep breath while I waited for them to answer.

"A thousand," Lu said quietly.

I poked my fingers into my eyes as I tried to get my mind around the fact that we had already committed to bring out a thousand people in a town whose entire population was just over eleven hundred. I sighed, shook my head, and said, "Okay. I'll contact Galen and ask Marcus's mom to get out a special newsletter tomorrow. What are you two doing for marketing?"

Mom pulled her purse off her lap and took out postcards. The front side featured an artistic rendering of Lu's own food truck, and the back had all the details of the event. "We're distributing these here in town and all the way over to Easton."

I took a card and held it up. "Cate did these for you?"

"One of her artists did." Mom smiled. "Stephen and Walter are coordinating the vendors with Lu's help, and Lucas is baking his brains out so we have lots of cupcakes to sell."

"So I was the last to know?" I wasn't sure why that bothered me so much. This wasn't my gig after all, but it did.

"Only because we wanted to be sure we had everything in place before we asked you to do one more thing for us," Mom said, squeezing my fingers tight. "Are you still in touch with Laura Lippman?"

I groaned. "Yes, but five days is very short notice—"

Mom interrupted me. "I know, but she lives over in Baltimore, right? It's not that far, and maybe she'd like the chance to do something casual and fun."

I sighed. "Alright. I'll ask. But don't bank on that, and please don't advertise it until we have details worked out."

"No problem. We've just told everyone there will be a special guest, so we can make that anyone we want." Mom was so optimistic, but I could just imagine a thousand people being markedly disappointed if I was the special guest, as it seemed might be likely if Laura wasn't available.

I had been fortunate enough to meet Laura Lippman at a mystery writers conference a few months ago. We'd hit it off in the restaurant one night and had stayed in touch casually. And by *casually* I mean that I liked her posts on Facebook, and once in a while she liked something I shared about the store. It wasn't exactly a deep and robust friendship.

But I knew Mom was right. Adult people could always say no to anything they didn't want to do, and so I got onto Messenger and sent Laura a message. "Any chance you'd be up for a small-scale charity reading for our local library this Friday?"

I was not expecting an immediate reply, but the three dots that meant she was typing came up almost instantly. "I'm in town and have no plans. Where and when?"

I stared at the screen for a minute then quickly typed a word of gratitude and all the details, using the card Mom had let me keep since I didn't even know the details myself yet.

"Great," she replied, "And before you ask, no honorarium necessary if I can stay at your house."

I took a deep breath. "Of course," I typed, trying to sound all casual. "Home-cooked breakfast on Saturday morning."

"Perfect. I'll come in about two on Friday. Text me the address." She included her phone number and a smiley emoji.

In the quick exchanges of notes, I'd lost track of Mom and Lu, but when I looked up, they were both grinning. "From the look on your face, I'd say she agreed," Mom said.

"Yes, she did, and she's staying at my house." I'd had the privilege of meeting several famous people, and a few of them had even come for other events here in St. Marin's. But no one had stayed at my house before. This was going to add a wonderful new level of stress to the weekend.

"Okay, that's settled, so now we can start promoting seriously?" Lu said. "What's our fundraising goal again?"

Mom smiled. "I say we go big, especially with a wonderful special guest. Ten thousand dollars?"

"Perfect," Lu said as she turned to look at me. "What do you think, Harvey?"

I was a bit dumb-founded honestly, but when I got my breath I said, "That's a lot of tacos."

Lu laughed. "Yes, yes it is."

The number of customers in the store had grown while we talked, so after telling Mom and Lu to let me know what else they needed help with, I went back to the floor to help Marcus answer questions and ring up sales. I would have to process the fact that one of my favorite mystery writers was coming to my house another time.

A few sales and a few YA title recommendations to a young man with a wonderful preference for all things Royal, including a deep love of *Caraval*, and I was delighted to find Tuck in a wingback chair reading *The Long Fall* by Walter Mosley. Typically the sheriff was much more of a literary fiction man, but I'd recently recommend Mosley's work as contemporary noir. Tuck had said he'd check it out, and here he was, a man of his word.

I dropped into the chair next to him, and he tore his eyes away from what must have been an exciting scene to look at me. "Lu run her idea by you?" he asked with a grin.

"If by 'run by' you mean 'steamroll,' then yes." I sighed. "It's a good idea, but I do wish we could plan something with a little more lead time at some point."

Tuck chuckled. "You won't get any arguments from me on that count."

I studied my friend for a minute before I said, "Lu didn't tell me anything except that you found Joe Cagle. I don't want to pry—"

"Of course you want to pry, Harvey. That's just who you are. I did find Cagle. He was holed up at a motel outside of town." Tuck took out his handkerchief and slipped into gently into the pages of the book to mark his place.

"Oh, wow. So he was hiding?" I asked.

"Yeah, but not because he was hiding from me. He was terrified." Tuck shook his head. "Wasn't making much sense, but I brought him to the station on the promise that he could stay in the cell with an officer nearby twenty-four seven until we caught Sidney's killer."

I frowned. "Cagle didn't kill him then?"

"I don't think so, but you know I don't rule anything out." He lifted one corner of his mouth as he said his usual refrain. "He's really scared, like he saw something."

"He saw Sidney be killed?" I was fishing here, and I knew it.

Tuck sighed. "I'm really not sure. I'm hoping that some good sleep, a good helping of Lu's food, and a sense of safety will calm him down enough to get a clear statement." He looked at his watch. "Speaking of which, I should check on him."

I stood with my friend. "It's your day off. Can't Watson handle it?"

"This from the woman who can't stay away from her own store on her own days off?" He winked. "I'll just be in there a minute. Assess Cagle's state."

Lu came up behind him. "That's right. One quick stop and then we're off to dinner and movie. You promised."

"I am a man of my word," Tuck said as he kissed Lu's cheek. "See you later, Harvey."

I smiled as my friends left and then let the panic over the fundraiser in under five full days rise up until I quelled it with my usual treatments of rapid action and lists.

By the time the store closed a few hours later, Mart was planning a breakfast of champions for Saturday morning, my dear friends Henri and Bear had agreed to take Laura out for dinner before the event on Friday, and Galen and Mrs. Dawson were on top of publicity through their usual channels.

Marcus and I closed up shop, and I headed home with two pups who were eager to sniff and pee on the entire world, it seemed. But a slow, leisurely stroll was okay with me since my brain felt a little overstuffed. I tried to quell my excitement and nervousness about Laura Lippman's visit by thinking about Sidney's murder. What I couldn't quite figure out was why Joe Cagle was so very terrified. He wasn't exactly a shrinking violet of a person, and physically, he was big and appeared strong. It occurred to me, as I walked, that Tuck hadn't told me the cause of death, but maybe the way Sidney had died had something to do with why Cagle was so scared. I almost let curiosity get the best of me and texted Tuck to ask, but I remembered it was his day off and thought about how stressed he had been. I let it go.

Mayhem, Taco, and I were just about to turn onto our street when I saw a flash of movement just to my right. I turned, expecting to see one of those very quiet electric cars driving by, but instead, I caught a glimpse of a light blue bicycle helmet and a reflective blue shirt. The bike had been very close, and I jumped back, even though the rider was far past me at that point.

I stared after it for a while, frustrated by their carelessness but also feeling a little tickle of something else – familiarity maybe. But getting all worked up wasn't going to help, especially since the bike was long out of sight and headed toward downtown. So I gave the dogs a gentle tug and let them lead me on toward home.

6

T hat night, Mart and I completely vegged out. We
didn't even make dinner but opted instead for an a la
carte menu of cold cuts, cheeses, and peanut butter
crackers. Her wine event had been a big hit with the giant
corporation from outside DC, and she had been asked to coordinate similar events for their clients over that way in the next
few months. The work was going to be good, but that much
small talk and strategizing always left Mart tired.

And with the big event coming on Friday, I really needed to
do something to distract my mind. So we opted for watching
The 100, a sci-fi show that was just enough drama and romance
to keep us occupied, especially while we let ourselves gawk at
the teenage hero Finn.

Four episodes and almost a whole jar of peanut butter later,
we let the dogs out, tidied the kitchen, and headed to bed,
where I found Aslan asleep on my pillow. She was less than
thrilled when I moved her over so I could actually lay down,
but I was so tired I didn't even care when she went back to sleep
on my neck.

. . .

THE NEXT MORNING, though, I woke up feeling revived and ready to go, which was good because when I picked up my phone at six-thirty, I already had three texts from my mother, all asking for me to call her as soon as I got up.

I recognized this kind of urgency brought on by her early morning planning stints and waited until I had a cup of coffee for stamina before I called her back. When I did dial her number, she didn't even say hello before she started asking for my opinion on whether or not we should get a liquor license for the event, how we should handle parking, and what kind of signage was necessary to direct the visitors.

As I sipped my coffee, I gave the appropriate "I'm listening" sounds as she worked her way around to her own answers. I got my need to verbally process things from my mother, and these calls were simply a way for Mom to talk through solutions she was quite capable of determining on her own. It was a new part of our relationship, one I actually treasured, even early in the morning, because we hadn't always been close. That I was the one she called and trusted to just let her spill out her thoughts felt special and good.

Fifteen minutes after the call began, Mom took a breath and said, "Thank you, Harvey. You are always so good at helping me think through these things."

"You're welcome, Mom," I replied with the first words I'd said since Mom first picked up the phone. "Happy to help. See you later at the store?"

"You bet. I'll bring the signs by mid-morning so you can tell me if you think they are easily readable from the road." She said her good-bye and hung up.

I smiled as I scrambled up an egg with cheese and washed some grapes. The signs would be perfect when Mom came with them, but I'd need to find some small suggestion that didn't require her to redo them, just so that she felt good about including me. Maybe I could offer a note about color, suggest some balloons or such.

The notion of color got me thinking, and I texted our friend Elle, who ran the local Farm Store and sold the most amazing cut flowers, to see if she could donate some bouquets for the picnic tables on Friday. Her reply came quite quickly because she, like Mom, was an early riser. "Absolutely. Your mom already contacted me about a bouquet for the library counter, but I'll do a few small ones for the picnic tables, too. Come by later and pick out some stems?"

I always loved going into Elle's shop because it smelled so good and because the flowers were so beautiful. Plus, Elle had become a dear friend, and it was only her gardening expertise that had kept me weeding and seeding in my own small plot of vegetables and flowers. That little garden had become a respite for me, and this morning, I slipped on my rubber shoes and went out into the dew-laden grass to stare at my tiny cabbage plants and the rosemary and sage that had wintered over so well.

I could see the leaves of my hollyhocks poking up in the small bed against the house, and I thought the foxgloves were beginning to show, too. Elle had wisely suggested I keep those separate from my food stores since they could be very poisonous. She knew that I was a novice gardener and didn't want me getting all experimental with edible flowers that might kill me. I appreciated her caution.

As I stared at the tiny first leaves of my flowers, something prodded at the back of my mind, but I couldn't quite grab it from where it was just beginning to grow in the folds of my brain. So I took another sip of coffee and headed inside to finish my coffee and see if Mart was up.

If I was my mother's sounding board, Mart was mine, and while she stood patiently and sipped her own first cup, I rambled on about foxgloves and poison and somehow found my way to talking about how scared Joe Cagle was . . . I knew there was a connection, but my thoughts kept interrupting themselves with the phrase, "Laura Lippman is coming to your house," and I couldn't put the ideas together.

Fortunately, the caffeine had activated Mart's synapses, and she said, "You think Sidney was poisoned and Cagle saw it happen."

I stared at her for a moment as the statement sunk in, and then I nodded, a little stunned at how clearly my friend had understood my verbal meanderings. "Yes, I think I do. Or at least I wonder if that's what happened. We didn't see any blood or anything, so I don't think he was hit or stabbed. I'm guessing the killer hoped people would think it was just a natural death . . ." My thoughts were spinning faster than I could catch them.

"Take a breath, Harvey," Mart said quietly. "What do you think Cagle could have seen if it was poison?"

I stared at Mart and blinked for a few seconds. She had hit on the key question. "I have no idea, but I think it's time I talk with Tuck again."

Mart nodded and smiled. "Your brain just can't let things go, can it."

I gave my head a little shake. "Apparently not." I glanced at the time on my phone. "I better hustle if I'm going to stop by the station before work."

Within a couple of minutes, Taco, Mayhem, and I were on our way, this time with far fewer pauses for pee and sniffs since I had a timeline to work with. Soon, I was tying them up by the bowl of water that the dispatcher left outside the station for passing pups and heading inside to talk to Tuck.

Our sheriff was very patient with my "curiosity," or what he called nosiness, but given how much stress he'd been under, I didn't know if he was going to love my visit this morning. I could only hope that his day off made him patient or at least gave him the resources to be kind when he told me to buzz off.

The young woman at the front desk told Tuck I was there, and he said I could come on back. As I walked the few yards to his office, I decided to use Mom's concerns about parking and traffic as a smokescreen for my real reason for visiting. I doubted that Tuck would buy it, but at least I would feel a little less intrusive. Maybe.

When I came in, Tuck smiled and said, "I wondered how long it would take you to come in."

I furrowed my brow and put on my best "whatever do you mean" look as I said, "You knew I would come in to talk about parking and traffic patterns for the Friday night fundraiser?" My voice was higher than usual, and I silently kicked myself for not practicing my lines before I came in.

"Oh, is that why you're here?" Tuck said with a smile. "Well, you'll be glad to know that your mother and I just spoke, and everything is set up in that regard. No need to worry."

I nodded and swallowed. Now that my smokescreen had been blown completely out of the room, I felt a little stymied.

"Was that all, Harvey? If so, and I don't mean to be rude, I have a killer to catch." Tuck gave me a serious look, but I could see the corners of his mouth bouncing.

"Okay, fine," I said with a pout. "I'm here to ask you what Sidney's cause of death was. I know it's none of my business, but I can't stop thinking about it."

Tuck's grin was wide and full. "I thought so. It took you long enough to ask."

"I was a little preoccupied by the fact that Laura Lippman is going to be staying at my house on Friday night," I said as a flutter of anxiety pounded in my chest at just the thought.

"Wow, that's great, Harvey. Maybe she'll come into the store and sign her books," Tuck said.

The pace of my heart picked up a tick more. "I hadn't even thought of that, but yeah. I need to get more copies of her books in." I glanced at the phone in my hand. Twenty minutes until I needed to open, and I had to get that order in this morning to have it on time for Friday.

"To answer your question, it wasn't poison. I can't tell you more, but that information will likely be common knowledge soon enough since I think Pickle might have overheard me talking about it with Watson when he was in visiting his client this morning," Tuck frowned.

Pickle was another good friend and a very good attorney. "Pickle is representing Joe Cagle?" As far as I knew, Cagle was the only person who would need legal representation at the sheriff's office, so it seemed like a good bet.

"Yes. Cagle has not been willing to tell us anything yet, although he was smart enough to ask for an attorney. So he's clearly not as terrified." Tuck ran a hand over his bald head. "Pickle's a good man. I expect we'll get some more information from Cagle soon."

I nodded and sighed. "I hope so. I hate to think of Sidney suffering while he lay there alone."

Tuck grimaced. "Yeah. It's not a pretty picture."

"I better go. Sorry to bother you, but you know me."

"I certainly do," Tuck said as he walked me to the door. "You care, Harvey. I know that. Just be careful you don't care too much."

I smiled and walked out the door. Caring too much had always been my problem.

As I WALKED with the dogs to the store, I tried to shake the image of Sidney suffering under that table from my head. I had long ago learned there was no value in dwelling on things I couldn't change, and fortunately, I was finally able to control my thoughts, at least a little bit. Walking helped soothe me, and when we got close to the store and saw our friend Galen and his English Bulldog Mack waiting outside, the day got even better.

Galen was my favorite customer, mostly because he was a wonderful person and a fellow dog-lover, but also because he was a great champion for my store. Surprisingly for a white man in his senior years, he had built up a huge Instagram following, and he used it often to promote the shop and the events we held. My financial stability was, in part, due to Galen's faithful sharing of what I was doing here.

"Good morning, Sunshine," I said as the three of us approached and the dogs did the rounds of sniffing each other's various parts. "You're out and about early?"

"I am. I'm out of books, and I have an idea to run by you," he said with a smile.

"Ooh, you know I always love your ideas. Come in. I'll just need to get the store opened up, and then we can chat." I unlocked the door and led our canine entourage in as the bell chimed above us.

"Perfect. Mind if I browse right away? I have some Lippman books to catch up on." He headed right for the mystery section, his favorite, and I got to the computer and ordered three copies of every book Laura Lippman had written as well as fifty of her newest release. I hoped that would be enough.

As soon as I finished turning on the lights and the open sign, I stopped by to see Rocky, who as usual had been here a while to get her café ready for the day's first guests. She and I had talked a little about hiring an assistant so she could stop working all day every day, and she wanted to do that but had her own financial figure in mind where that would be viable. I hoped she reached that goal soon because I wanted her to have some kind of life outside of the store.

The bell over the front door rang again, and I turned to see Marcus coming in right on time, a huge smile on his face and his skateboard under his arm. When he saw me his smile brightened, but when he saw Rocky, he practically shone.

I glanced back at her and sighed. Maybe it wasn't so bad that she was here every day. She seemed to like the company.

Greetings done, I headed over to the mystery shelves to find Galen and see if we had what he needed to complete his reading of Lippman's oeuvre. Galen was, like me, a completer when it came to books. He rarely gave up on a title even if he didn't enjoy it, and he liked to read a series in order whenever possible. Normally, he was a cozy mystery lover, but he also appreciated any kind of intrigue, well, any kind of book really. I think that's why he felt like a kindred spirit; our love for books ran deep.

When I found him and the three dogs tucked in and around a club chair near the mystery titles, he was already deep into the third book in Lippman's Tess Monaghan series, *Another Thing To Fall*. He smiled at me briefly before returning his eyes to the page, and I took the universal hint of readers everywhere and left him be.

Marcus and I had gotten out most of the new releases the night before, so all we had to do for this, my favorite book day of the week, was freshen the display table at the front of the store. We did that quickly, moving a few less-well-selling titles to the back or onto the main shelves and sliding the new ones into the prime spaces. I was especially excited to read *The River Has Teeth* by Erica Waters, a YA fantasy with a mystery at its heart, and I set aside a copy for myself.

I didn't buy a lot of books these days because my budget didn't allow it and I wanted to keep our stock for customers because I wanted to please them and, if I'm honest, because they paid full price and I didn't. But sometimes a book caught my eye, and I knew I wanted to have my own copy to read. If I loved it, it would go onto my shelves. If I just enjoyed it, as I did most books, I'd donate it to our library or put it in a Little Free Library when I was done.

My chores finished, I spent the next little while perusing the shelves for returns, a job I hated but one that was necessary to keep my shop from being buried in the financial weight of unsold titles. I was just about to cull from the self-help shelves when Galen found me and asked if I had time for a latte.

"I always have time for a latte," I said as I checked in visually with Marcus to be sure he was solid. He smiled, and the three dogs trailed Galen and me to the café. I tried to buy our drinks, but Galen insisted and so with my free latte in hand, he and I took a table by the window.

I was dying to know what Galen had to share with me, but I was also Southern enough that I needed to do my best with small talk for a bit. "You doing okay?" I asked.

He nodded. "Doing great. Had my physical last week. Clean bill of health." He grinned. "Okay, so I'm on TikTok now."

I laughed. "Of course you are." This particular social media phenomenon was totally lost on me, just as Snapchat had been. I was fully ensconced in the middle-aged world of Facebook and content to stay there, but I loved that Galen was branching out.

He smiled. "I've started doing book reviews there, and they're taking off." He took out his phone and showed me an article about how young book reviewers were launching titles onto the bestseller's list with their honest, often tearful reviews of books on TikTok. "It's super easy and really fun, actually. Mack even makes cameos."

I was not in the least surprised by this bit of dog-related info given that Mack had a very popular Instagram following himself. "That's wonderful, Galen. How can I help?"

"Oh, I don't need your help, Harvey, although I appreciate the offer. What I need is a bookish space to film a few times a week? I thought the store might work." He raised his eyebrows and looked at me hopefully.

I stared at him for a minute and then said, "You want to film videos here, live, in my store? Like while we're open or after hours?"

"Oh while you're open. Each video is about one minute long, and the ambiance of the store will be great. No need to worry if I'm interrupted or anything. I just want to have good internet to do them, mine at home can be spotty for video, and bookshelves behind me. You won't need to do anything at all." He took a sip of latte and watched me over the rim of the mug.

My first instinct was always to say yes to everything, but I'd finally begun to learn to pause, think, and then answer. So I took my own sip of my sweet beverage, looked out the window for a few seconds, and then asked my question, "I love this idea, Galen, but I have to say that I really don't have space or energy to coordinate anything. Do you really mean I won't have to do a thing, not even steer customers away from where you're recording?"

He smiled. "I totally understand, Harvey, and you won't need to do a single thing. In fact, I won't even let you know when I'm coming. That way, you can't even try to prepare. I'll just come in, sit down, and record." He took a deep breath. "But also, you can say no, and I won't be offended at all."

I sipped a few seconds more and then I said, "I love this idea. Please use my store." I smiled and felt the excitement I'd been holding back a bit for the sake of caution rise up.

Galen tapped his hands on the table in excitement. "Great, and of course, I'll talk about the store and tag it in my videos. My hope it that it'll bring in more customers for you, too."

I reached over and took his hand. "Friend, that would be great, but really, I'm just glad to be able to help you after you have done so much for us" I stood up. "Now, though, I need to go sign up for TikTok so I can watch your videos."

He laughed and stood, too. "Before you do, mind ringing me up?" We strolled toward the register, and I saw a teetering stack of paperbacks waiting at the end. "I have a few things to purchase."

As usual, his total was huge, and I gave him as I always did, the employee discount. He was, basically, our press team, and even if he wasn't, he bought in such volume that I would have felt inclined to give him the discount anyway.

We said our goodbyes, and Marcus helped him and Mack carry his purchases to the car while I checked out the gaping holes in the mystery and thriller sections and upped my order of Lippman's books. If I knew Galen, he'd be in soon to review his reads of her titles, and I expect that would mean quite a few more sales. I just hoped they'd arrive in time for Friday.

The rest of the morning passed easily with customers in and out and a few phone calls about Friday's event since Mom had listed the store number as the main contact. It was looking like the turnout would be great, and I hoped we raised a lot of money in Sidney's honor. Of course, that part I wasn't worried about. My mother had *never* missed a fundraising goal, even if she had to kick in the difference herself.

Around noon, I took my lunch break and decided to settle on a bench overlooking the stream by the library to eat the sandwich I'd packed. I could feel the sadness over Sidney's death finally creeping in, and I wanted to honor my feelings while also paying him a small tribute of attention.

I grabbed the dog's long lead lines and headed out with my reusable lunch bag that Mart had scored at some wine convention. I loved the thing because it kept my sandwich cold and meant I didn't have any trash to throw away when I was done. Also, it kind of reminded me of having a lunch box, something I'd loved when I was a kid. Mine had been covered in Shirt Tails, a short-lived cartoon that I had loved when I was little. I wondered if Mom still had it. Probably.

I found a nice sunny bench that would allow me to see the stream, watch the joggers going by, and give the dogs plenty of space to roll and tumble on their leads without tripping anyone. With them tethered to the leg of the bench, I opened my bag and smiled at my lunch of a ham and cheese sandwich, chips, and a fresh, super-dill pickle. Something about this meal made me happy. Maybe it was the simplicity, maybe some sense of nostalgia for the days when I was working as a fundraiser in San Francisco and couldn't even afford to buy a drink if I wanted to pay my rent. Whatever it was, I loved this food, and I savored every bite even as I thought about Sidney and how tragic it was that he had died.

Taco and Mayhem tumbled around together for a brief time, and then they sprawled out on their sides in the sun and slept hard. I know because they both snored, much to the delight of everyone who walked past. I took out my e-reader and dove back into *Midnight at the Bright Ideas Bookstore*. I was so engrossed in my reading that I jumped when someone sat down next to me.

Out of instinct, I scooted over and grabbed hold of the dogs' leashes, but when I looked up, it was my friend Pickle with his own brown bag lunch in hand. "Sorry, Harvey. Didn't meant to startle you. I forget how you get with your books."

I blushed and shook my head. "Sorry. It's good to see you. Perfect day for a lunch outside."

"I agree . . . but I have to admit I was actually looking for you. Marcus said you might have come this way." He took a sub out of his bag and studied it before taking a bite.

"Oh?" I figured this must be about Joe Cagle, but why Pickle would look for me I had no idea.

He finished his mouthful and swallowed. "I need your help." He took another bite from his sandwich and chewed thoughtfully. "Cagle is innocent, but he's too scared to tell Tuck what he knows."

As he took another bite of his sandwich, I sighed. At this rate, it would be mid-afternoon before I got the details, so I decided to try and fill some in for myself while Pickle ate. "You think I could convince him to talk to Tuck?"

Pickle nodded and continued to eat.

"And you're sure he didn't kill Sidney?" I knew that was a dangerous question to ask an attorney about his client, but before I'd agree to participate in anything, I needed his confidence that he was representing an innocent man.

After wiping his mouth with a napkin, Pickle looked me dead in the eye and said, "I do. I know it's my job to defend him no matter what, and I do my job well, no matter my personal beliefs about my clients' guilt or innocence. But in this case, I really do believe he didn't do anything but be in the wrong place at the wrong time." He winced slightly as if he'd said too much.

But I nodded. "So he did see who killed Sidney?"

Pickle's face was completely neutral. "You know I cannot reveal anything he said to me, Harvey, but I think he would talk to you. Will you see if you can get him to share what he knows with Tuck?"

I sighed and for the second time that day forced myself to pause and consider the request. A murderer was on the loose. A witness was too terrified to talk. A friend was asking a favor. It was pretty much as easy a choice as letting Galen film in the store, just with a lot higher stakes involved. "Okay, but I want you to be there. I don't want him telling me anything that might get him in trouble because I can't promise not to tell Tuck what I learn if Joe won't."

Pickle grinned. "Exactly what I was hoping you'd say. You free now?"

I glanced at the time on my e-reader. The after-school rush was still over an hour away, so I nodded and took out my phone to text Marcus and let him know I had to run an errand. Then

Pickle and I gathered our things, untethered the dogs from the bench, and made the few blocks' walk to the station.

When we came in the door of the station, Tuck was standing straight and rigid in front of a very large man in a fedora. The guy looked to be about six feet six, and under his silver hair, his pale skin was bright red with what seemed like anger given how loudly he was shouting. "I want to talk to Cagle, now. He's shirking his contract to work on my house, and I need that bathroom finished this week."

I caught Tuck's eye, and he gestured with his forehead to tell us to wait where we were.

"I'm sorry, Mr. Reeves, but Cagle is in my custody. He cannot leave, and you may not speak to him. Your bathroom will just have to wait." I could see the muscles in Tuck's jaw flexing as he stared the larger man down.

"You think you're going to win this election when you treat your constituents this way, Sheriff Mason? I doubt it."

"Mr. Cagle is also my constituent, sir. Now, please, leave." The sheriff stepped toward the man, and for a second, I thought Reeves might punch the sheriff. But he looked briefly at Cagle, who was watching from the cell, at the receptionist, and then back at the two of us and thought better of it, probably because Pickle had taken out his smartphone and was filming the whole thing.

"Fine, but I will find him when he gets out. Don't doubt that," Reeves said as he spun toward the door.

"The law doesn't take kindly to threats, Mr. Reeves," Tuck said.

"Oh, that wasn't a threat. Simply a fact," the large man said as he turned back in the doorway. "I don't say things I don't mean, Sheriff." Then he strode out onto the sidewalk and away.

Pickle looked from me to the sheriff and then strode right over to his client. "Joe, are you okay?"

Cagle nodded and then said, "I hope you understand now."

The sheriff walked over to the cell. "I do, and I think it would be better if we got you to a more private location. I know you can't go home, but we can find you a safe house."

"I may know somewhere he can stay," I said quietly.

"He cannot stay at your house, Harvey," Tuck answered.

"I wasn't thinking that." There was a little defensiveness in my voice because I had thought of it briefly but dismissed it because I didn't feel comfortable, for once, having a stranger – a second stranger really – in my house. "I have a guest coming this weekend, so that's not going to work anyway. What about Stephen and Walter's place, Tuck?" I suggested.

Tuck looked at Pickle, and Pickle took a minute to consider the idea. "They're fairly isolated out there, and as far as I know, they've had no involvement in this case, right?"

I sighed. "They were there when we found Sidney's body, but after that, no."

Cagle said, "I don't know about this."

"I know you're scared, Joe," Pickle responded. "But I think the sheriff is right. It's too public here, and you obviously can't go home. If Walter and Stephen agree, I think that could work." He turned to the sheriff. "Make the call."

I started to take out my phone, but Tuck stopped me. "I need to do this officially, Harvey." His voice softened. "Thanks for the idea."

I smiled. "Of course." I looked back at Pickle. "Maybe we should have this conversation later, when Joe is settled?"

Pickle nodded. "I'll be in touch."

I smiled, tried to give Joe Cagle my kindest look, and headed back to my shop. I was glad the dogs were out front because I felt a little unnerved by Reeves' behavior and didn't want to run into him alone on the street. Secretly I hoped Mayhem and Taco had tried to take a bite out of his leg as he went by. I doubted it, but allowing myself that tiny bit of imaginary justice felt good as I walked back to the store.

When I walked in, I was surprised to see my mom and Lu at one of the café tables. They had tiny pieces of paper spread in front of them and were deep in conversation. As curious as I was about what they were doing, I decided to leave them be and spend a little time decompressing from the events at the police station by straightening some shelves.

We didn't have a large poetry selection, but I always made sure we carried a few titles from both popular poets, the current poet laureate, and local writers. When I needed a quiet few minutes, this was a quick and easy section to put to rights, and the satisfaction of seeing orderly books always eased something in me. Fortunately, the shelves were a bit of a mess today, which meant someone had been browsing heavily, and I could see that several spaces on the shelf were empty.

With the shelves tidied, I scanned our inventory and saw that, indeed, we were due to order a few poetry titles back in, including the beautiful collection, *African American Poetry: 250 Years of Struggle and Song*. I'd added the book to our collection as soon as it came out because I loved the poetry of Kevin

Young, the editor, and from time to time, I'd dipped into the pages, letting the rhythm of words fill me. I hadn't read the whole book, but I did savor the poems I spent time with. Since my shop was in a former gas station that had at one time been listed in *The Negro Motorist Green Book*, it felt right and important to honor black people in every way I could, even if I only had a few minutes to do so.

I placed the order for the titles we needed and then noticed Marcus talking to a little boy in the children's section. The boy's clothes were a little ragged, and I saw that he had just a few crumpled dollar bills in his hand. I scanned the store for his parent, hoping that this wasn't another time when someone thought the bookstore was a good place to leave an unattended child, and was pleased to see a smiling woman nearby. She too looked a little worn, but she seemed happy, joyful even, as her son talked books with Marcus.

While I pretended to straighten the counter so that I could watch Marcus and his new friend, I saw them go to the picture book shelves and study a few titles. Eventually, the boy seemed to settle on one, and they brought it to the counter. The book was a delightful story called *Slow Samson* about a sloth who is always late to his friends' parties.

As the boy approached, Marcus met my gaze and held it, and a kind of silent communication that we had developed in our months of working together passed between us. The boy slipped the book onto the counter, and then he laid his three dollars and eighteen cents up there, too. The book cost well over fifteen dollars even with Marcus's employee discount. But Marcus knew that I, almost as much as he did, wanted to foster a love of books in the young.

"It's your lucky day. There's a sale on this book, and the cost is exactly $2.18. So you still have a dollar." The boy beamed and looked back at his mother who mouthed a quiet thank you to me when he turned back to gather his change.

"You two have a nice day, and enjoy Samson's story. It's one of my favorites," I said.

Marcus walked mother and son to the front door, and when he returned, he tried to hand me the balance for the book from his wallet.

"No sir," I said as I put up my hand to stop him. "As of this minute, we now have a children's book fund for just such situations. If either you or I see a child who wants a book but can't afford it, we take what they can give and credit the rest quietly to them. I'll set aside a couple hundred dollars a month for just that purpose."

Marcus smiled. "I like that idea, Harvey. Thanks. I hope you don't mind . . ."

"I loved what you just did, Marcus. Thank you." I thought for a minute. "And if we don't use all the funds in any given month, will you coordinate a book giveaway by buying books to give away with the remaining dollars?"

My kind-hearted assistant manager swallowed hard. "I would be honored. Maybe Mom could note it in the newsletter?"

"Definitely. You take care of the logistics, and we'll plan on the first day of each month to do a small book giveaway for children who come in." I didn't know exactly how we'd manage the influx of kids and the limited number of titles we'd have, but I trusted Marcus to sort that out.

With the store fairly quiet and Marcus riding his kindness high, I took a minute to step over and check in with Mom and Lu. When I approached, they each looked up and smiled. Then, Mom said, "How does this look to you, Harvey?"

I stared at the slips of paper on the table and said, "Are you planning a flotilla?"

Mom scowled at me. "We're trying to organize the food trucks so everyone can get in and out easily."

I smiled. "I figured, Mom. But this is good practice if you

ever do a benefit involving boats." I studied the arrangement. "It looks good to me, but you know that spatial reasoning is not my forte."

Lu laughed. "Mine either, but I do know how to drive a food truck. I think this layout gives us the space we'll all need to maneuver and give customers room to queue up for food."

"Looks like it to me," I said as I studied the design again. "Is there room for me to have a table to sell Lippman's books? I figured that might be a nice gesture since she is donating her time."

"Agreed. We've set up a space for you right here," Mom said as she pointed at a small square right near the entrance to the library.

"Cool," I said, "but I guess the really important question is how close am I to Luke's cupcake table?"

Mom grinned. "He's right here." She indicated the table next to mine, and I laughed. "Perfect. The sugar high will keep me going all night."

For the next few minutes, the two women walked me through the plan for Friday, and it sounded amazing. Laura Lippman would speak or read, her choice, for just a few minutes, and then, the next morning, if she agreed, she'd sign those books here at the store. Food would be served before, during, and after her talk, and Mindy had agreed to open the library so that the book sale could happen at the same time.

Quietly, Lu also told me that Henri and Bear were creating a memorial piece of art to unveil that night. Henri was a talented weaver, and I knew that whatever she created would honor Sidney well and be a lovely addition to the library.

Everything sounded perfect, and my only job was to ask Laura if she was willing to sign books at my store the next morning. I texted her to ask, and she agreed readily. "You need to benefit from this, too," she wrote.

I smiled. "Thanks," I replied and then did a panicked call to my distributor to see how many copies of her books he could get me by Friday. Fortunately, he was happy to oblige and drop-ship an additional hundred books to arrive on Friday morning. I placed the large order with his assurance that, as always, I could return any copies I didn't sell or want to stock, a great boon for a small indie bookstore like me. I then collapsed back onto the stool in relief.

FOR THE NEXT couple of hours, Marcus and I did our thing, selling books, suggesting books, and straightening shelves. We were just busy enough that I had to focus entirely on the store, which felt amazing given how scattered my thoughts had been with the fundraiser and the murder investigation.

Still, when it came time to close up shop, I did so gladly and looked forward to a few hours at home to simply relax with Mart and eat a good meal. Fortunately, Taco and Mayhem seemed just as eager as I was to get home, and we took a casual but direct walk home, where they then played in the yard like puppies before passing out on the patio.

It was a lovely night, so I poured a glass of wine and sat down in the evening light to wait for Mart, who was bringing home Thai food from our favorite place in Annapolis.

The song birds were just beginning to dance around our feeders, and I could see the first leaves coming out on the trees. Someday Mart and I wanted to landscape back here, make it a real garden oasis, but for now, it was just a nice lawn with a couple good shade trees. It was enough, tonight, to help soothe my frayed nerves.

I almost ignored my phone when it rang, but given all that was going on, I didn't think it responsible to skip even one call. It was Pickle with an update to let me know that Stephen and Walter had gladly agreed to shelter Cagle with regular police patrols checking in. "It's a good thing, and Joe seems more at ease now that he's not in the center of town."

"That's good," I said and braced myself for what I knew was coming.

"Do you think you could come tomorrow and talk with him, Harvey? I thought maybe Walter and Stephen could get him to open up, but he hasn't."

I sighed. "Okay. But if he's not willing to talk to the two kind men who took him in, I'm not sure he's going to be forthcoming with a woman he's never met."

To say I slept fitfully that night would be a massive understatement, but when I woke, I decided I was going to do my best to help Cagle trust me, mostly so that I could help Tuck. Although, I knew Tuck would not be thrilled I was doing this, both because it might put me in danger but also because it was really his job, not mine.

Still, it didn't look like Cagle was going to talk to the actual police, so maybe I could do something, get some information for Tuck that he couldn't get for himself. That's at least what I told myself when I loaded Mayhem and Taco in the car and gave Aslan a can of tuna and the house to herself. She looked almost ecstatic.

The drive out to Walter and Stephen's place was always beautiful, but with the fresh spring green on the grasses and trees, it was particularly lovely. I found myself relaxing and enjoying the rare few minutes of time I had to listen to my current audio book, *Little Bookshop of Murder*. It was a great read because it was, of course, about a bookstore and, of course, a mystery. But I could only read it in short bursts because it felt a little too close to home sometimes. Thus, it was the perfect audio book for me, who only got in her car once or twice a week.

When I pulled into my friends' driveway, I was tempted to keep listening to my book for a while, but I knew they'd already seen me and I didn't want to look like I was avoiding my obligation, although now I really wanted to do that. Suddenly, this seemed like a very bad idea.

Still, I had made a commitment, and whenever I could, I did what I'd said I'd do, another reason I was getting more and more careful about saying yes.

Stephen opened the door and immediately pulled me into a hug as he whispered, "You can still change your mind, Harvey." He pushed me back and looked in my face. "You look tired."

Only a friend as dear as Stephen could say something like that to me without it being an insult, but he cared. And I knew he was telling the truth. "I am tired, but I'm here. So let's do this." I looked around and smiled at Walter, who was cooking up a feast in the kitchen if the smells were to be believed. "Tell me you have coffee."

Stephen rolled his eyes. "Of course. I have your vanilla latte all ready to froth." He headed for their cappuccino machine and got steaming.

Cagle and Pickle were sitting at the island across from Walter, and they both looked relaxed, much more refreshed than when I'd seen them yesterday at the sheriff's station. I tried to muster some enthusiasm as I said, "Good Morning, Gentlemen. I see you're strategically positioned to get the bacon just the way you like it."

Joe actually smiled and said, "I'm not a demanding person except when it comes to breakfast food. I like my bacon crisp and my eggs runny."

I grimaced. "And I'm the opposite. Pull my bacon off soon, but let those eggs get good and dry for me, okay Walter?"

Walter saluted and tightened his apron around his belt. "If I ever need a job, this is good practice for being a line cook." He smiled and flipped the bacon over before removing three pieces to a paper towel.

I slid into the remaining bar stool and grasped the pottery mug that Stephen handed me with both hands. Patience was not one of my strong suits, so I just decided to delve in. "Mr. Cagle, I know you don't know me, but I'm hoping you might tell me what you know about how Sidney died."

Cagle turned toward me and said, "You don't think I know you, Ms. Beckett, but I know everyone here in St. Marin's a little. Nature of my job and my life, I guess. You've done a good thing with that bookstore, and the events you've held have helped a lot of people."

As I sipped the latte that was almost as good as the ones Rocky made, I took a deep breath and continued. "Well, thank you. I try to do what I think is right whenever I can, which is why I'm here. I'm wondering if you can help find who killed the librarian. Our friend Sheriff Mason isn't one to admit he needs help, but for this, he kind of does."

"He's up for re-election, isn't he?" Cagle said.

I sighed. "Yes, but—"

"And they're giving him hell because he's black." Cagle said it as a statement not a question.

"Yes," I said with relief that my presence here wasn't going to be read as political. "They are."

Cagle reached over and snagged a piece of bacon right off the griddle and chewed on the crispiest end. "You asked her to come," he said to Pickle.

I looked at his attorney and my friend beyond him at the counter, and Pickle nodded. "I did. Harvey is a good listener, and she's the one who found Sidney. Plus, anything you tell her she can tell the sheriff without compromising your case."

When I glanced over at Walter and Stephen, they were laying the food out on plates on the counter. Neither of them looked the least bit bothered that this man who was staying in their home wasn't willing to confide in them. I admired their generosity and open-spirits so much.

As we all made plates and gathered around the farm table with the view of the water, Cagle told us what he'd seen. "I was coming into the library, and I saw Reeves in his huge, blue pickup leaving the library. I came in my usual way, through the trees at the back, so I wasn't sure he saw me." I must have looked puzzled because he said, "I prefer walking the trails rather than the sidewalks."

"But yesterday, you came to think he did?" I asked between bites of delicious scrambled eggs.

He nodded. "I didn't really think much of it at the time, but then, when I came in the library, I saw that young woman with blonde hair take something off the table in the back. She was acting all secretive. Looking around and sliding whatever she'd picked up into her pocket. Then, she went the long away around to get to the counter at the front, and I couldn't help thinking she didn't want anyone to see her coming from that direction of that table."

Stephen asked, "Did she see you?"

Cagle shook his head. "No. Most people don't notice me, and I was between the tall shelves looking for a book on gardening without tilling the soil. Trying to preserve the life under the ground, you know."

Joe Cagle was, as far as I knew, American born and bred, but in his phrasing, I picked up just a hint of Ireland or rural England, maybe. It gave him a quaint air that took some of the edge of his brusque appearance.

I wiped my mouth with my napkin. "Mr. Cagle, what do you think about what you saw on Saturday? Why did you hide and then run?"

Cagle looked down at his plate and sighed. "When you live like I do, reliant on other people's trust and thoughtfulness to survive, it's important to not draw negative attention to yourself, especially when you think you saw something nefarious, you know?"

I thought that over for a minute. He had a regular job, but clearly the gas station attendant gig wasn't enough if he had to depend on odd jobs to make ends meet. I didn't know that experience because I'd always had steady work to keep up my way of life, but I could see what he meant. "You figured you'd seen something people didn't want you to see, so you pretended to not see it."

He nodded. "Aye. I'm not proud of it, and if I had known Sidney was dead, I would have come forward right away. I just figured I was witnessing some kind of illicit liaison or something."

Walter leaned forward, "Between Lucy and Reeves?"

Cagle shrugged. "Maybe. Seems like that's possible now, but at the time, I didn't think anything of Reeves much, just that young woman being so cagey and all." He sighed. "When you found Sidney's body, I just didn't want to be involved." He looked at each of us in turn, and I felt the effort required to hold our eyes for even a few seconds each. "I'm sorry," he whispered.

I reached over and took his hand. "We know." I didn't understand his instinct to hide. I seemed to have the opposite one and was always getting myself involved in things I probably shouldn't. I did understand the guilt of having done something you now regret. "I don't think it made any difference that you didn't come forward right then. Sidney was already dead."

"Yeah," Cagle sighed. "But it might have meant we caught whoever did this sooner."

Pickle patted his client on the back. "Maybe. But we have the information now, and you have a safe, warm place to be until the sheriff catches the killer."

I looked at Pickle and then Cagle and said, "If it's alright with you, I will go tell the sheriff what you told me. He'll want to talk to you himself, but I expect that can wait if you need to regroup a little, Mr. Cagle."

Cagle shook his head. "I'll be ready whenever he is. Now that I've shared it once, it doesn't seem so scary. It feels safe here, too." He smiled at Stephen and Walter, who beamed.

"Not only safe, but fun. We have a *Lord of the Rings* marathon to get to, my friend," Walter said.

"I've never seen those movies," Cagle said to me, "and since I can't really work, garden, or beach comb, seems like as good a time as any."

I stood up. "Mr. Cagle, that sounds like a perfect day to me. Thank you."

Pickle walked me to the door and gave me a quick hug. "Thank you, Harvey. If you would, please ask Tuck to come out soon. He'll know to be discreet, but I think the sooner we can get Joe's statement on the books, the better."

I nodded. "I'm on my way there now." I waved to everyone and walked down the steps to my car.

As I climbed into the driver's seat, I felt a little scurry up my neck, like someone was watching, but I didn't want to look nervous if that was actually the case. I pulled out without swiveling my head and just tried to keep my eyes straight ahead as I pulled away. I didn't see anyone, but the sensation didn't fade until I was down the road a bit.

WITH ABOUT A HALF-HOUR until the shop opened, I texted Tuck and asked if he could meet me at my store. "But come in the back," I said.

"Be there in two." When he arrived, I let Tuck into through the back door of the store, and while I did my usual opening chores, he walked with me. "You didn't want me to be seen coming in?" he guessed as he helped me restock the front tables with the most popular titles of the week.

"Not after I just came from Walter and Stephen's," I said, impressed by his intuitiveness. "Cagle told me what happened."

Tuck sighed and nodded. "Okay. We'll talk about your decision to visit him later, but for now, what did he say?

I relayed what Cagle had told me about what he saw at the library and then I told Tuck about Walter's theory that maybe Reeves and Lucy were in a relationship.

"You mean she's "Sweet Sugar?"" he asked.

I shrugged. "I have no idea, but it's a possibility I guess." I handed Tuck a dust rag, and he graciously dusted shelves alongside me. "I don't even know if Reeves being there and Lucy taking the note are related. It's just a guess."

Tuck carefully ran his rag along the front of the fiction shelves as he said, "Looks like I need to talk to both Reeves and Lucy. He should be easy to bring in without tying anything directly to what Cagle told you, given his outburst at the station yesterday."

I nodded. "Right. Good." I folded my own rag – one of Mart's old running socks – and said, "Have you located Lucy yet?"

"No, not yet." He shook his head. "She's local. Even went to Salisbury for college, but I haven't gotten any leads on where she is hiding away. Her mom seems to be as clueless about her whereabouts as we are."

"Maybe she's really scared like Cagle?" I suggested, not wanting to think ill of the lovely young woman who did such great work in the children's section of the library.

"Or maybe she's a murderer," Tuck said grimly as he stood on a stepstool and wiped the top of the bookshelf in front of him.

8

Tuck graciously stayed and helped me dust the rest of the store, so when the doors opened at ten, the shelves gleamed and I felt unburdened. I had no doubt the sheriff and I would have a conversation soon about me inserting myself into another investigation, but for now, I felt good that he knew everything I did and that he might have a little more to go on in catching whoever killed Sidney.

I had also let him know about my sensation about being watched at Stephen and Walter's, and he had decided he'd boat out to their house later that morning on the pretense that he needed to liaise with Fish and Game about illegal harvests on the river. Given that we were a water town, I knew that Tuck had access to a boat, but I'd never seen him on it. Somehow, though, the image fit, and I wished I could go along for the ride. I hadn't yet had the opportunity to sail along the river on that side of town, and I loved the water. Today, though, I was needed at the shop, especially with the fundraiser coming up in just two days.

Soon, I was very glad I'd stayed, too, because we got a call from *The Baltimore Sun* about the event, and I was eager to answer questions and get the free publicity in tomorrow's paper.

The store was also hopping, and when Marcus came in at eleven, I breathed a little sigh of relief. A group of mothers had come in unexpectedly to ask if they could hold their book club, right then, in our fiction section and let their children, with their hired babysitters, browse in the children's area. "Of course," I said outwardly even as I groaned inwardly. There were eleven children on hand, and while the babysitters managed them well, I knew that we'd have a massive clean-up when they left. I just hoped I didn't have to pick up dirty diapers as I had done a few times.

The women, though, were reading *Rules for Being a Girl*, and so I was already predisposed to like them. Any group of moms who were confronting patriarchy were good with me. I even found myself recommending that they do their club here every month and offering a discount on their selection if they bought it from me.

The women were enthusiastic, and when they ordered nine copies of Ibi Zoboi's *Pride*, I was so thrilled they had come in that morning, even as I could see the disaster that was the picture book section from the register. That disaster was a small price to pay, though, when most of the women ate lunch in the café and then came back to the shop to browse and buy. I was always glad to have new customers, and thoughtful readers like this made me especially happy.

The afternoon flew by, and about three when Mom and Lu came in with the streaming banners they were going to put alongside the road to the library to help folks find the event on Friday, I realized I was starving. I needed something to eat and to get off my feet. Lu had to get back to her truck, but I asked Mom if she'd go to Max's with me for a salad. I still wasn't ready to face him alone, but I knew Mom would be a good buffer if the situation got tense.

As soon as we walked in, Max greeted us himself, and while he gave me a small smile, he didn't say anything except ask if we wanted the lunch or dinner menu. Lunch menus in hand, he led us to a table in the window and then disappeared into the back to let his waitstaff take care of us for the rest of the meal.

I ate a delicious spinach, walnut, and feta salad, and Mom ordered some stuffed mushrooms and a raspberry iced tea and we both spent the meal making sounds of delight with each bite. Max wasn't the man I wanted to spend my life with, but I could spend my life eating in his restaurant for sure, that was if I could work up the courage to explain myself.

Fortunately, I didn't have to do explaining today because Max didn't come back out. I heard him in the back talking with someone, and for a second, I even thought I heard him laugh.

But I was more focused on telling Mom all about what I'd learned from Cagle this morning. She was, of course, quite interested. Dad was always polite when I told stories, but Mom was engrossed, especially when it came to what my dad called my "snooping." It was clear from whom I'd inherited my curiosity.

"So he saw something but doesn't know exactly what he saw?" Mom asked.

"Yeah, we think so. Clearly, he thinks he witnessed something he shouldn't, but what he saw exactly is the big question now." I sighed. "I'm sad about the whole situation."

Mom took my hand. "Of course you are. Anyone's death is a sad thing, and Sidney was a fellow book lover. That would make anyone sad."

"Thanks, Mom." I sighed and forced a smile onto my face. "Let's talk about something fun. How's the planning for Friday coming?"

If ever I wanted a distraction from my own life, I only had to ask my mom about her latest project, and I could delve into the details just by following the trail of her enthusiasm. Today was no exception. She was delighted about the small stage that the high school choir director was going to loan them for Laura's reading, and the fact that the local news stations were coming had her overjoyed. "It's going to be a big deal, Harvey, and I have you to thank."

I laughed. "Are you kidding? This is all you, Mom. I sent one message, but you and Lu have done everything else. I can't wait to see what Mindy decides to do with the money you raise."

Mom got a mischievous grin. "She's already got some plans. Want to hear what they are?"

"Of course," I said and leaned forward. But I didn't get to hear what Mom had to say because just then someone stepped up to our table and cast a shadow over it.

In the split second before I looked up, I took a deep breath, thinking it was Max come to clear the air, but when I lifted my eyes, I was shocked to see Reeves towering above us. I couldn't get my words out because he looked like he wanted to wrap his huge hands around my neck and choke me.

Fortunately, my mother is never at a loss for words, and she said, "Can we help you?"

Reeves flicked his eyes to Mom and then back to me. "I need to talk to you, Ms. Beckett." His voice was quiet, but somehow that was even more intimidating.

I found my spine and said, "I'm having lunch with my mother just now. You can find me at my store later."

The man actually growled. "Now."

Just then, I saw a hand reach up and grab Reeves' shoulder in an attempt to turn him around. Reeves frowned and then looked over his shoulder. "What do you want?"

"Sir, these women are enjoying their lunch. I'd be happy to get you a table if you'd like, but if you are simply here to harass them, I'll need to ask you to leave," Max said.

I suppressed a smile both because Max looked so stern even as Reeves dwarfed him in size but also because Max was still being kind to me, even after I'd treated him horribly.

"Would you like a table?" Max repeated.

Reeves shook his head and then looked back at me. "I'll be at your store. Don't keep me waiting." Then he stalked out the door and toward my shop.

I took a long deep breath and grabbed my phone. "I need to warn Marcus," I said.

Max already had his phone to his ear. "Tuck, you are needed at Harvey's shop." Max looked at me. "A man – Harvey what was his name?"

"Reeves," I said.

"A Mr. Reeves was just here at my restaurant intimidating her. He's waiting for her at her store." Max paused to listen to Tuck and then said, "Thanks."

I sent my text, and Marcus replied immediately. "Got it. Tuck on his way?"

"Yes," I texted. "You're not alone, right?"

"No, Rocky and Galen are here. See you soon."

I stood and Mom took out her credit card to pay the bill. "Thank you, Max," I said. I was about to explain, briefly, my behavior toward him when our waitress returned with our check.

Mom handed her the card and then made herself busy with a hunt through her purse that rivaled the most intense archaeological expedition in the world.

"I'm sorry, Max. I know we need to talk, but maybe not today," I finally blurted.

Max took my hand in his and kissed it, but not in his old, creepy way. This time, it was sweet and kind . . . and very platonic. "We don't need to talk, Harvey. I understand that I was there at a time when you needed support, and I'm glad I could be."

I smiled and suppressed the tears that threatened to spill over at his kindness. "Thank you for understanding."

The waitress returned and handed Mom the slip to sign.

"Besides, I've met someone." He turned toward the waitress and put out his hand. "Harvey, this is Mel." He took her hand in his. "Mel, this is my friend, Harvey. She owns the bookstore down the street."

I grinned. "Mel, it's very nice to meet you." I wanted to say something about her having a good man, but I felt that was a little over the top. "Come into the store sometime. I'd love to get to know you."

Mel smiled. "Thanks, Harvey. I'll do that."

Mom stood. "Thanks for lunch, Max. As always, it was delicious. Harvey, we probably need to get down there," she said.

I cleared my throat. "You're right. Thanks, Max, and again, nice to meet you, Mel." I would have lots of time later to feel the relief that my avoidance of Max hadn't made things completely awkward between us, but for now, I needed to attend to a possible murder in my bookstore.

9

M om and I walked as quickly as we could back to the store, and I was relieved to see that Reeves was sitting in the café with a mug of something. He looked up when we came in, and I held up one finger to tell him I'd be right there. Mom wandered off into the cookbook shelves, where she could keep an eye on me but not look conspicuous.

Then, I made a show of checking in with Marcus, looking at the computer screen intently, and doing a quick walk around the store as if it was my usual routine. I spoke briefly to Galen and Mack, who were browsing in the mystery section, and Mack trotted along behind me as I wandered on. I was just about out of reasonable ways to stall when Tuck and Watson walked in.

Tuck caught my eye as I fluffed a throw pillow on one of the wingback chairs in the front window, and I flashed my eyes over to the café. He gave me a subtle nod, and then headed toward the racks of greeting cards I had at the front. He and Watson made a show of looking for a perfect card for their receptionist's birthday, and I appreciated the presence and the subtlety, clumsy as it was.

Apparently, my nerves were showing because as I headed toward the café both Mayhem and Taco pried themselves from their beds in the window and joined Mack as the three lumbered after me. As soon as I sat down, the three dogs settled at my feet protectively. I knew they weren't asleep, and if Reeves did anything untoward, Mayhem would have her teeth on his arm faster than Tuck could even pull his gun. My own canine security detail.

"What can I do for you, Mr. Reeves?" I asked as I sat down and smiled when Rocky brought me a latte and a nod to show she also had her eye on the situation.

"You know where Joe Cagle is." He didn't ask and his voice was brusque and cold. "Tell me where I can find him."

Reeves' back was to Tuck and Watson, and I didn't know if he'd noticed them. But they moved just the slightest bit closer, to hear but also to move in if needed. At least I hoped they were ready to move in.

"I don't know Cagle , much less where he is," I took a deep breath and hoped my lying skills were improving. "But now you have me curious? I heard you in the station saying you wanted to talk to him because he was in the middle of a reno job for you. But this," I waved my hand around between us, "feels like more than that. Why do you want to find this man so much?"

A tiny furrow appeared on Reeve's broad forehead, but I couldn't tell if that was because he believed me or because I was starting to annoy him. "Please don't give me that bull about not knowing who he was. I saw you with his attorney at the police station."

I smiled. "Attorney? Oh, you mean Pickle. He's a good friend. We were there to ask the sheriff to get breakfast with us." I tilted my head and just barely refrained from batting my eyes in my attempt to sell my line.

Reeves practically spit on me when he huffed. "Fine. Play it that way. But I'm going to find him." He stood up so abruptly that his chair fell over behind him. "And if that means I have to stay close to you to do it, that's just what I'll do."

He spun around toward the door and only hesitated slightly when he saw the sheriff and deputy watching him. Then, he was out the door and into his pickup across the street, leaving black tire marks on the road when he spun out.

Everyone rushed over, and I slumped back into my chair. "You handled that so well, Harvey," Rocky said as she put her hand on my shoulder.

"Yes, you did, sweetheart," Mom said as she sat down across from me. "What did he say?"

Tuck and Watson waited to hear the answer, too, and Marcus and Galen stood a bit away, listening as well. "He just wanted to know where Cagle was. I obviously didn't tell him, but I don't think he believed that I didn't know."

"You need to be sure you're not alone for a while, Harvey," Tuck said. "I don't think we can put a protective detail on you because of our staff limitations, but I want you to keep me posted on where you are at all times. And no being alone."

I'd heard this caution from Tuck before, and I'd shrugged it off because I was convinced I could take care of myself. That hadn't gone so well, so I took his advice seriously. "I won't be." Then I looked around at my friends. "Potluck at my house tonight?" I said with a smile.

"I've got the steaks," Mom said.

"I'll bring the salad," Marcus added.

Soon even Watson was volunteering to bring over some fresh asparagus, and Mom had texted everyone else to invite them and suggest they bring sides. It was going to be a hearty meal, and that felt like just what I needed after this day.

Once the crowd had dispersed and the dogs had gotten their biscuits of gratitude and returned to their beds, I spent a few minutes talking books with Galen. He had snapped some photos of Reeves and was ready to disseminate his picture via social media if need be. "You are a good friend, Galen," I said.

"Just doing my part, Harvey." He turned back toward the shelves. "Now, what should I be reading now?"

Normally, this question thrilled me because I loved recommending books, but Galen was far more well-read in the mystery genre than I was, so I was always a little bit stumped. Still, I wanted to try. "You've read all of Lippman's catalog already haven't you?"

He grinned. "Yep."

"Okay, so you're all set for Friday." I turned back to the shelves. "What about VM Burns? Are you familiar with her work?"

Galen's smile got even wider. "I am not. Tell me more."

I pulled *The Plot Is Murder* off the shelf. "It's a bookshop mystery, so I love it."

He took the title from my hands and then pulled the rest of the series off the shelf, too. "I'm all set for the next few days. Thanks." He, his stack of books, and Mack all headed to see Marcus at the register, and I took a deep breath of delight at the open space on my bookshelf. Time to go see what I had in backstock to fill in the hole.

I spent the next few hours climbing up and down the wonderful library ladder that my friend Woody had built me as I grabbed books and fleshed out the titles on the shelves. Marcus recommended books to customers and staffed the register, and when closing time rolled around, we were both singing. He was rapping some Lil Nas, who I liked but could never do justice in my own voice, and I was bopping about singing like Bob Dylan. "There must be some way out of here. . ." The mash-up wasn't really a smooth one, and soon, we were both laughing as we closed up, grabbed Rocky, and headed on foot to my house.

Marcus had arranged for Elle to meet us, and we added her to our dog and person entourage at the corner. Rocky had decided to bring along a carafe of decaf coffee as her contribution, and so we wafted a delightful fragrance as our crew of middle-aged, white women and young black people was led along by two sniffing hounds.

When we arrived at the house, Mart and Symeon, her boyfriend, were already staffing the grill, and Mom and Dad were setting up folding tables and chairs in the backyard. I hadn't thought about eating outside, but it really was a great night for it – warm and calm. Marcus and Rocky headed toward the kitchen to make the salad and set up the coffee, and I followed behind hoping I still had the bag of chips and the jar of salsa that I intended to add to the night's offerings.

Mart had brought wine for everyone, and soon Henri and Bear arrived with an amazing couscous salad that included olives. Cate and Lucas brought the "scratch and dent" cupcakes from the batches he was making for the fundraiser on Friday, and Tuck and Lu carried in a tray of hot churros for dessert. When Watson came with his asparagus and Walter and Stephen brought in a bowl of hot, creamy mashed potatoes, I almost swooned with delight. Immediately, though, I wondered who was with Cagle, and Stephen said, "We left him to a *Lost* binge and with our cell numbers. Apparently, he's never seen the show." Walter rolled his eyes and turned back to our other friends who had, apparently, better taste in television.

Soon, the food was set out on the island in the kitchen, and everyone was circling round and talking while they filled their plates. I took the chance to ask Symeon about Max's new girlfriend, Mel, and Symeon grinned. "They are a good pair," he said but then studied me for a second. "You okay with that?"

I smiled as I added another spoonful of mashed potatoes beside my steak, "I'm more than okay with it. I'm very happy for them both."

"And relieved," Mart added before looking at me. "Right?"

"Right," I said and headed back outside to eat.

We all laughed and talked about life and work and the fundraiser on Friday. Everyone was coming, of course, and Mom made sure each person had their assignments. Apparently, Cate was doing her usual papier-mâché magic and making a large book to display by the library front door to encourage people in, and Walter and Stephen suggested a donation for parking and said they'd take care of directing cars and collecting the two dollars a vehicle if people wanted to give.

Henri and Bear were going to be Lippman's hosts, and I couldn't imagine a better pair for the job given how they knew everyone in town and were naturally friendly people. Mart and Symeon were going to be doing tastings of the winery's best – to anyone with a wristband that showed they were twenty-one, and Marcus and Rocky offered to manage checking IDs and distributing the bands.

It was going to be a great night, but I couldn't quite get my enthusiasm all the way up since all of this was only happening because Sidney had been killed. When a lull developed naturally in the conversation, I leaned over to Tuck next to me and said, "Do you mind if I crowdsource a bit?"

Tuck sighed. "You mean about what Cagle told you?"

I nodded. "I know it's not your way, but I'm wondering if anyone will have ideas – and since he told me . . ."

"You can share whatever you want that Cagle told you, Harvey." He sighed again. "Just remember to let people know about your encounter with Reeves, too. They need to understand the dangers of getting involved."

This time, I sighed and said, "Right. Thanks." Then I stood up and clinked my fork against my glass. "I need your help, everyone."

Every eye in the yard turned toward me, including the six canine ones, although Cate and Lucas's dog Sasquatch looked like he could barely keep his eyes open after all the tumbling he, Mayhem, and Taco had been doing.

I quickly told them about what Cagle had seen at the library, and Walter immediately joined the conversation. "So we think there's some connection between Reeves and Lucy?" He looked to Tuck.

Tuck shrugged. "I am not a part of this conversation. We're just having a very nice gathering with friends."

Watson snickered and then took a sip of his red wine. "Right. Just chatting with friends." He smiled at his boss and then sat back to listen, too.

I knew that Tuck was never happy with my involvement with his cases, but I also knew that he'd learned it was better to just let me – and our friends – do our thing than to try to keep us away. At least, then he knew what we were up to.

"Alright, so brainstorming. Let's go," Stephen said as he took a pen out of his pocket and prepared to make notes on the white paper tablecloth Mom had spread out. "Reeves and Lucy. How might they be connected?"

Mart spoke up first. "Could they have been, um, lovers?"

"Lovers?" Bear said with a grin. "Is that the term we're using?"

"Okay, dating," Mart said with a blush.

"A possibility," I said. "That could mean that Lucy was 'Sweet Sugar.'"

"Or Reeves was," Henri said with one eyebrow raised.

"Ooh, that's good," Mom added. "So they were together, maybe?"

Stephen drew an arrow with a question mark over it on the tablecloth. "That's one possibility. What else?"

Dad said, "Could they be connected other than romantically? I mean Reeves is, from what you said, Harvey, old enough to be Lucy's father."

Lucas hissed. "Well, that's a new twist on things." He shuddered.

"A sort of unsettling one given what our first guess was," Watson added before Tuck gave him a quick look to tell him to stop talking.

Watson shrugged. "Sorry, I got caught up in the conversation." Then, he made a gesture like he was locking his lips.

"What if they're not connected at all?" Symeon asked. "Maybe it was just coincidence that Cagle saw Reeves and then watched Lucy take the note."

Elle spoke quietly. "Right. Reeves is acting awfully squirrely, but maybe he's just very angry about the state of his renovation. It's only Lucy who was witnessed doing something really shifty that was directly related to Sidney's death, right?"

I sighed. "Well, and Cagle running, but yeah." I paused. "Okay, let's back up and review what we know. I found a note near Sidney's body that mentioned Mary Roach's book *Stiff* and the inside back cover."

"Then, we saw Lucy try to destroy a note at the pier," Mom added.

"We assumed that it was the note that was in the book," I said as I shook my head, "But maybe that's not the case."

Walter cleared his throat. "Maybe we didn't find what was actually in the book you mean?"

I nodded. "Maybe? But the note is still important."

Stephen wrote furiously and then tore a big section from the tablecloth. "So we have this theory about Lucy and Reeves being connected. But it's based on some assumptions that we can't prove."

I looked around and saw my friends nodding as Stephen continued. "But what we really know are these three things: Reeves and Lucy were both at the library."

"Cagle, too," Mart said.

Stephen added to his note and then continued. "We have a note mentioning, we think, something in the back of a book."

Tuck interrupted. "A book Mindy Jackson was trying to hide."

Watson looked at his boss and smirked. "Hard to stay quiet, isn't it?"

Tuck glared at him and then looked back at Stephen. "Keep going."

Stephen jotted a note about Mindy and the book and then held his makeshift whiteboard up for us again. "So we know four things: the first note in Sidney's handwriting; the second note in an unknown hand; Mindy hiding the book; and Reeves, Lucy, and Cagle at the library at the same time."

"And Lucy trying to destroy the note," I added.

"And Reeves threatening Harvey," Marcus said firmly. "Let's not forget that."

Stephen grabbed his pen and jotted down three names before ripping the tablecloth again and holding up the list of our suspects. Lucy, Mindy, Reeves.

I groaned. "So we're no closer to knowing what's going on than we were." I put my head down on the table.

"I wouldn't say that, Harvey," Cate said as she moved over and began to rub my shoulders. "We know that someone called Sidney to ask him to find something – the note or something else – in that book. At least that seems the most likely interpretation of his own words, right?"

I looked up and watched my friends nod again.

"So whatever he found put him in danger," Cate continued.

"We need to find what he was looking for," Rocky finished.

Tuck cleared his throat. "I need to find it, you mean." He stood up and held his hand out for Lu. "It's my job, folks."

Lu smiled at her husband, and I realized that she hadn't said a word throughout our conversation. She was clearly showing her support and faith in Tuck, and I felt a little bad that it looked like we didn't have faith in him.

I stood and reached my hand out to the sheriff. "And you will. I have no doubt."

Tuck smiled, but it looked forced. "Thanks, Harvey. Now, all of you, keep an eye on our bookstore owner, okay? She's not to be left alone until this case is solved."

Mart stood up and wrapped her arm around me. "I'm on guard duty twenty-four seven."

I looked over at her. "But you have to work?"

She shook her head. "My bosses gave me the next two days off to help with the fundraiser, which I can do from your store."

I squeezed her. "Well, I don't think I need a guard," I paused when Tuck groaned, "But I'll appreciate having you around. "

"We'll all be around," Mom said as she stood and began to clear the table. "Rocky, mind if we commandeer a table in the café as our headquarters for the next two days?"

"Not at all, Ms. B," Rocky said with a smile. "I'll keep you supplied with coffee and snacks."

"And I have some reading to catch up on," Dad said as he stacked our plates to carry into the house. "I'll be on hand for anything that needs attention."

I swallowed back the lump in my throat and looked at my friends. "If the rest of you say you're going to be in my store, too, I may have to get more furniture." Everyone laughed.

As we went about the last steps of clearing the table, tidying the kitchen, and loading the dishwasher, Tuck and Lu came over. "Thank you, Harvey," Tuck said.

His face looked strained, and once again, I thought about how hard this all was on him. "I wasn't doing this for you, Tuck," I said and realized right away how harsh that sounded. "You don't need our help, I mean. I did this for me because I can't stand unanswered questions."

Lu gave me a small nod, and I knew I'd said the right thing.

"You've got this, Tuck." I looked over his shoulder to where Watson was helping Elle fold tables. "And you've got a great sidekick."

Tuck laughed. "I may have to get the cap and pipe yet."

THE NEXT MORNING, Mart walked me to work, despite my attempts to get her to sleep in by assuring her that Taco and Mayhem were sufficient guards for the walk. "Those two would surely defend you, Harvey, but they aren't exactly the visual deterrent that might be needed."

I couldn't really argue with her because my two canine companions were fierce protectors guised in the bodies of goofballs. So we each had a pup for our walk and took our time as we enjoyed the spring morning. Two of our neighbors were retired and spent most of their time working on their landscaping, and so the walk by their yards was always a visual and scent-filled delight. Today, we marveled at the colors of their purple tulips and coordinating hot pink azaleas, which were blooming up a storm. One of them had also put in an arbor at their front walk, and the scent of jasmine wafted over us as we brushed against the vine. Someday, our yard would look like that.

Today, though, we had enough to worry about with the threat Reeves had made toward me and the fundraiser coming up in less than thirty-six hours. Sometimes I felt a little overwhelmed by all that I got myself involved in, but on days like today, when fear could take over, I was always glad for the distraction of hard work.

And hard work was definitely the name of the game that morning since half the copies of the Lippman book order were being delivered to the back door when we arrived. Fortunately, Marcus had come in early, so he had opened the door for the delivery truck. Now, the two men were working hard to upload the twelve cartons of books that had come in.

I stared, a bit stupefied by the sheer number of volumes that were being unloaded, but then Mart reminded me that Mom, Galen, and Mrs. Dawson had been marketing this event massively and that it would be a boon for the store when we sold all the copies. I didn't mention that I had another order of almost equal size coming the next day, but I sure hoped I hadn't overdone it.

Fortunately, my guard detail arrived just as we opened, and I put Mom to work with Marcus designing the new Lippman display for the front tables by the door. I was glad I had, too, because people came by to pick up copies of her books all morning, and by noon, our supply was already down by a third.

I had wisely held back about half of the shipment for tomorrow night's event, and I was now very glad I had more books coming the next day. Still if we ran low, I knew I could special order in anything if people couldn't find what they needed, and I decided I'd ask Laura if she'd come to a special event later in the year to read and sign at the store. That way, people would be able to get their copies signed if I ran out of books this weekend, a possibility that looked more probable every time I rang up a sale.

In the early afternoon, Mindy Washington came by to check on planning and to let us know that she had put up her own Lippman display if people wanted to borrow rather than buy. "I have a copy of each of her books in hardcover and many on audio, too," she said.

"Oh good," I replied. "I know some folks who can't afford to buy or who prefer the environmentally wise option of borrowing or listening. I'll add a sign to the display to let people know you have those choices available."

"Thanks, Harvey," she said. "I wanted to also show you something, if you have a minute." Her quick glance around the store told me we might need to move somewhere a little more private than our more-busy-than-usual front counter.

"Sure, want to step into the back room?" I waggled my eyebrows to highlight the silly suggestiveness of my joke, and Mindy laughed.

When I had closed the door to the storeroom, I suddenly realized I had just done what Tuck had promised I would not do – I was alone with one of our suspects. I couldn't do much about that at the moment, but I did make sure I stayed close to the door.

Mindy reached into her small purse and removed what looked like an old-fashioned snapshot, like the ones Mom had in photo albums from my childhood. "I found this under the nonfiction shelves nearest the tables where Sidney died when I was vacuuming yesterday."

She handed me the picture, and I looked down at it. The image was of a young, blonde girl and an older man, someone maybe her grandfather's age, and they were both smiling for the camera. The little girl had a Raggedy Anne doll, and she was hugging it tightly. It was a very sweet picture.

But something about it was needling me. I couldn't quite put my finger on what was concerning me, though, until Mindy said, "That's Lucy, I think."

I looked more closely at the little girl, and sure enough, it was definitely possible that the child was the other librarian. "It does look like her. But it's hard to tell. What do you think this girl is, four or five?"

Mindy nodded. "Yeah, I'm thinking so. And because she's wearing Power Rangers stuff, I'm thinking it's the nineties. I looked it up, and Power Rangers was released in 1993."

"So the girl is the right age to be Lucy, too." I sighed. "We need to take this to Tuck."

"Yeah, I wanted you to see it first, though, be sure I wasn't overreacting. Maybe it's someone else's picture." She looked at me like she was hoping she was wrong.

"Well, that depends. How often do you find photographs under your shelves when you are vacuuming?" I asked with a half-smile.

Mindy shook her head. "Never," she said with a smile and a sigh. "I'll take it to the sheriff now."

"Good idea." I opened the door to the storeroom and caught Marcus's eye. He frowned and shook his head when Mindy and I walked out, but he didn't say anything. The rush of customers seemed to have let up for a minute. "Let me tell my friends I'm taking lunch, and I'll walk over with you, okay?"

"You don't have to do that, Harvey," she said.

"I'd like to," I said as I headed toward Marcus.

Marcus watched me approach and shook his head again.

"Sorry. I know. I didn't think when we went back there," I said before he could lecture me. "She found a picture of someone who looks like a young Lucy. She's going to take it Tuck, and I'm going to go with her."

"Great," Mart said as she appeared at my side. "I'm starving, and we can go get lunch after we walk her over." She looped her arm through mine before I could object.

So it was that the three of us and two dogs headed down Main Street. We tried to make small talk about the fundraiser the next night, and I was glad to see that Mindy was excited, not overburdened, by the plans. But eventually, we fell into silence brought about by the weight of that tiny photo in Mindy's fingers.

When we got to the station, the receptionist called Tuck right out, and when he saw the three of us, he invited us all back. "I think Mindy has got this one, Tuck," I said. "We're on our way to find Lu's truck."

Mindy glanced at me, a hint of panic in her eyes, but I knew she'd explain things well to Tuck. More, though, I needed Tuck to know that I didn't need to be involved in this conversation because I trusted he had all of this under control.

I hugged Mindy quickly before we left and said, "Someday you're going to explain to me why the librarian vacuums, right?"

She laughed. "Nothing to explain. It's one of my favorite things to do and gives me such a sense of accomplishment. We have a cleaning service, but I ask them not to vacuum just so I can do it."

Mart smiled. "I totally get that." She grabbed my arm again. "Now, let's go. I need tacos."

Tuck gave us a wave as we left, and he and Mindy headed to his office, the photo held out between them.

10

I pounded two of Lu's chicken mole tacos and didn't pass up the free churro she offered when I was done, even though Mart tried to make me look unhealthy by ordering a taco salad in an actual, not a fried tortilla, bowl. "Some friend you are," I joked as she grinned at me.

Back at the shop, Mart returned to a corner of the history section to do a little of her work for the winery, and I gave Mom a wave at her own table covered in paper and devices in the corner of the café. I laughed to myself about the idea of charging them rent for our shared workspace as I straightened the Lippman table again.

"We've been selling her books steadily," Marcus said as he brought a few more titles out from the back. "But I think we'll have enough to sell here tomorrow even without breaking into our stash for tomorrow night, especially with the order you have coming in the morning."

I nodded and told him about my idea of inviting Laura to do another signing in a few months.

"Good plan, but maybe you should check with her about

that so that we know if we can make that promise before we do it," Marcus suggested.

"You're right. I'll text her." I headed back to the register to shoot off my message and, again, got a reply almost immediately. She readily agreed and would ask her publicist to contact me about a date. She seemed confident we could find something since she could, as I suggested, stay with me again that night and make the drive back to Baltimore less than twenty-four hours later.

With that squared, I spent a bit of time getting special order forms made so that we could input the orders after the weekend when things would be a bit slower around the shop. Between that process, answering Mom's questions about Laura's books, and the steady stream of customers who wanted recommendations and decided to make purchases, I was zonked by the time it came for us to close.

Normally on Thursday, I might have gone home early and left Marcus to close up, but with the event tomorrow and the need to be constantly "attended," I decided to stay on and suggest a cereal and popcorn dinner to Mart. She was completely on board, so at seven, when we locked the doors, I was ready to veg and watch TV with a cat, a couple of pups, and my best friend.

Of course, the night before a big event was not going to be a quiet one. We had to clean the house and get the guest room ready for Laura, and our yard needed to be mowed. Knowing that I actually enjoyed mowing for the same reason that Mindy enjoyed vacuuming, Mart gave me the privilege, and I spent a surprisingly relaxing hour on our riding mower listening to a book Galen had recommended when I handed him Burns' bookstore cozy. *Little Bookshop Of Murder* was another bookstore murder mystery, and it was quite fun, especially since it took place in a beach town.

My daily dose of Vitamin D achieved, the yard looking

lovely, and the house looking and smelling great, thanks to Mart's liberal use of lavender-based cleaning products, we settled in with bowls of Cinnamon Toast Crunch and very liberally buttered popcorn. Our show of choice for the night was *Ted Lasso*, which everyone in the world had recommended as the feel-good option that we couldn't miss. One episode in, and we were both laughing and crying. It was the perfect show for the night, except for the fact that we didn't want to turn it off and go to bed when we should have.

I did manage some self-control before we started a third episode, though, and got myself to bed by eleven. Seven a.m. was going to come early, and I needed a good night's sleep to be prepared for tomorrow and I knew I wouldn't sleep much the next night with Laura Lippman in my house.

Unfortunately, the fact that I had been threatened on the week that a world-famous author was coming to stay with me only sunk in just as I started to drift off, and then I couldn't sleep at all. I thought about texting Tuck to ask if we could have a protective detail for one night while she was here, but then reconsidered when I realized that might derail any hopes of friendship I had with this woman, not to mention making her very ill at ease.

Rather, I decided I'd ask Mart if Symeon could stay over on the couch the next night. I didn't think he'd mind, and his presence as a chef the next morning for breakfast would be a huge bonus. With that hopeful thought, I eventually drifted off.

THE ALARM SOUNDED, and I jumped out of bed immediately, already wired for the day. I tried to slow down a little in the shower and enjoy the hot water, but I was too anxious to get to the store.

Because she knew me, Mart had gotten up as soon as she heard my alarm and was showered and waiting in the kitchen with bacon and egg sandwiches for us to eat as we walked to the store. "Thank you," I said as I gave her a quick hug. "I'm already kind of a wreck."

"You care, Harvey, and that's a good thing." She slipped her tote bag over her arm and dropped my messenger one over my shoulder. "Now, let's get to that store of yours and get the day started right."

I held up the sandwich as she locked the door behind us. "Bacon is always the right start for the day, right guys?" I looked at the two dogs who were, ever hopeful, waiting to get a piece of bacon.

"Don't let them fool you. They each had their portion already. I don't withhold bacon from any living creature," Mart said.

As we walked, I told Mart that I hoped we'd have a good turnout tonight and that I was eager to hear Mindy's plans for the money we might raise.

The corner of Mart's lip turned up when I said that, and I looked at her. "You know what she's going to do with the money?"

"I do, but I've been sworn to secrecy." Mart said and picked up her walking pace.

I pouted. "Why do you know, and I don't?"

"Because I am an integral part of the planning and you are a woman with a business to run."

"That doesn't seem fair." I was frustrated. "Who else knows? Mom I suppose? And Lu? Marcus?"

Mart wouldn't look at me, and my heart sank. "I'm the only one who doesn't know aren't I?'

"Trust me, Harvey," Mart said as we turned onto Main Street. " It will be worth the wait when you find out, and you won't have to wait much longer." The smile on her face grew as she looked down the street.

I followed her line of sight and saw a large banner flapping over the door to my shop. I couldn't read it yet, but given the small crowd of my friends outside, I figured something big must be going on.

I walked even faster, resisting my urge to jog over, but then stopped short when I saw what the banner said, "The Beckett Literacy Program for Children."

Around me, a few cars beeped their horns since I had stopped right in the middle of crossing the street, and Mart took my hand and pulled me out of traffic. "Surprise," she said quietly in my ear.

"What is this?" I asked.

"This is what we're raising money for, Harvey," Mom said. "It was Mindy's idea."

I looked around and found Mindy amongst my other friends. "You're starting a literacy program at the library?"

"We're starting a program," she said and looked at my parents, "in your honor, Harvey."

I stared at the banner and then at Mindy and back at the banner. I clearly wasn't processing what was happening.

Mom came over, put her arm around my shoulders, and led me inside to a table, where a display of materials about the program were set up. The brochures and cards all had a blue accent that sat somewhere between royal and teal, my favorite color, and each was labeled, The Beckett Literacy Program. I tried to read what they said, to understand what was happening, but I couldn't quite grasp what the words meant.

Dad pulled out a chair and gently pressed my shoulders into it. "Harvey, we've been planning this for a long time as a way of honoring the work you have done with your store and for this community, a community we now love, too." His voice was quiet as he knelt beside me.

"When your parents approached Sidney about organizing the program with the library a couple of months ago, he was very excited. He'd been working hard to set up a schedule and planned to use the library for one-on-one literacy tutoring," Mindy said as she sat down in a chair across from me.

Sidney's name jarred something loose in me. "But the money from tonight was supposed to benefit the library in Sidney's honor." I looked at the faces gathered around me and felt a profound weight in my chest. I was both honored and terribly sad, more sad than ever, about Sidney's death.

"It will be," Mom said as she rubbed small circles on my back. "We're dedicating Henri's art piece to him at the event tonight, and the tutoring room is already named for him. The sign is being hung today."

I took a deep breath and then smiled when Rocky set a mug in front of me. "Drink, Harvey. You look a little peaked," she said.

The mug was warm in my hands, and I let it settle me for a minute as I sipped and studied the materials in front of me. Then, I twisted in the chair to really see who was there and almost cried when I saw that all the people I most cared about were there. "You all knew about this?"

"We are better at keeping secrets than you are," Tuck said with a smile. He was right. I was a terrible secret keeper, a fact that I actually took pride in because I hated secrets, except for ones like this, which were really gifts more than secrets.

"Apparently," I said. "Thank you all." I wanted to stand up and hug each one of them, but I was still feeling a little too wobbly for that. "So how is this going to work?"

Mindy grinned. "All your friends and a few more people from the community have already been trained as literacy tutors. Some will specialize in helping adults, some children, and everyone has gotten instruction on helping people with learning differences like dyslexia."

I stared, open-mouthed, at the librarian. "All this happened without me knowing?" I knew that wasn't the central point of what they were saying, but I considered myself a pretty observant person and felt a little stunned I hadn't known or even suspected something was going on.

Mart laughed. "We aren't with you all the time, Harvey."

With my eyes wide, I took another sip of my latte and nodded. "Go on."

"Tonight's fundraiser will give us the means to advertise and train more volunteers, and next week, we'll begin the program in the Sidney Scott Room of the library," Mom said. "We've got a schedule set for after-school tutoring, and we're offering two mornings a week of training for adults."

Cate stepped up and said, "We even decorated the room so that if the students feel embarrassed about needing tutoring, they will have a sense of privacy while they work. You'll have to take a look this evening."

I shook my head again. "I just can't believe this, but I'm honored. I see a lot of people here in the store who struggle to read." I had always been puzzled by that fact since it seemed like only people who could read would come into a bookstore in the first place. But over the years, I'd come to realize that people love books, and they like to be around them, even if they can't read what's in them. I'd sat with people on more than one occasion to help them puzzle through something they wanted to find in a book but couldn't read themselves. I felt privileged to be trusted with that experience, and I'd always wanted to do more.

"That's where we got the idea, Harvey," Mom said. "A few months ago at dinner, you told us about a man who came in and wanted to learn more about the history of St. Marin's but couldn't read the books himself."

I remembered that man. He must have been about seventy with skin the color of walnut bark and a silver shock of hair. We sat together on a rainy Sunday for about two hours while I showed him the pictures in the books from our local history section and read him the names of people whose children he had known. It was one of my favorite memories of the store, and now I did remember telling Mom and Dad about it over soup at their house that night. "We will have to find him and offer him tutoring if he wants it," I said quietly.

"We will," Henri said. "But now, we have big things to do today, so let's give Harvey a minute to digest and get to work."

My friends scattered to various parts of the store to get us ready to open, to straighten the Laura Lippman table, and to, apparently, set up a volunteer sign-up space here in the café. Mom stayed with me, though, and sat down. "You okay with all of this, love?"

"Okay with it? I'm thrilled. Just spinning a bit as I try to catch up. I really can't believe it, but maybe we should name it in Sidney's honor, not mine," I said as I met her gaze.

"No, Harvey. Sidney wanted it named for you because of all the work you've done for this community. We are honoring his wishes by naming it for you." Her voice was firm but kind.

I let the tears that had been threatening to fall slide down my cheeks. "Okay," I whispered and then, "Thank you."

Mom took my hands and squeezed them tight. "Harvey, thank you. You have done a remarkable thing here in this store, and you do it out of kindness, not some desire to get rich off books. You are an inspiration."

Now, I was really crying because my mom didn't talk like this, not to me. Still, I could tell she meant every word she said. "Thank you, Mama." I stood up and gave her a hard hug.

Suddenly, all that needed to be done today, plus more now that this was a fundraiser for "my" program, came rushing down, and I was fired up. "Let's get to work. What do you need me to do?"

Mom grinned. "Let's take care of your business first, and then Galen will be here just after you open to film you for a promo on his social."

I laughed. "Did you just say, 'his social'"?

Mom's eyes grew wide. "Did I not use the term correctly?"

"No, you did. Just never thought I'd hear you utter that phrase." I smiled and headed into the store.

Since we'd come in really early, we had plenty of time to do a complete restocking of the shelves, clean the entire shop floor and the breakroom, and load Laura's books into the trunk of Mom and Dad's car for delivery to the event tonight. It was when I was putting the last box into the car that I had a staggering revelation. "Laura doesn't know what all this is about. I don't want her to be blindsided or feel like I didn't tell her something. Maybe she'll feel like I duped—"

Mart took the box from me and smiled. "She knows, Harvey. She's really excited."

I stared at my best friend for a minute as understanding bloomed in me. "You took my phone."

She grinned. "Took might be too strong a description. *Glanced at* is probably more fitting." When I scowled, she said. "I just got Laura's number one evening and texted her to introduce myself and let her know about the program. She really was thrilled."

I tried to act angry, but I couldn't keep my smile off my face. "She was, really?"

"Yes, really. She's offered to help spread the word for us tonight during her reading." Mart hugged me. "It's all under control, Harvey. We've got this."

As I walked back into the store, I forced myself to relax and trust that my friends really did have all this managed. I wasn't particular good at that, letting go of control, but I was really going to try today.

So when Henri told me I needed to sit down so she and Cate could do my hair and makeup for Galen's filming, I bit my tongue and just did it. Soon, my curls were tamed into a cute but still wild shape around my face, and I had on just enough blush, eye makeup, and lip gloss to make me look like my pale skin had some color to it. I looked good, if a little more "done" than I would normally.

Right at ten, Marcus opened the store, and a larger than normal stream of customers poured in. Many went right to the Literacy Program table, where Mom sat, and signed up to volunteer, and a few folks stepped into the quiet corner where Lu had put up a small sign that read "Get Tutoring." I smiled. We were off to a great start.

Galen and Mack came in and greeted all of us, including Taco and Mayhem, who led the Bulldog to the front window for some prime snoozing time in the limelight of the customers.

Fortunately, Mom was also planning on being on the video with Galen, and so while he asked me questions about why I thought literacy education was so important and what I hoped for the program, questions I could answer with little prep, Mom managed the information about the program itself, about our fundraiser, and about how people could donate. Apparently, the program was already registered as a nonprofit, so she was able to give a website and information about donations.

By the time the short video shoot for Instagram and TikTok was over, I was even more impressed by all the work that had gone on, and I really wanted to see the website. I grabbed my laptop from behind the register and cued up the URL. It was a simple tasteful site that featured a picture of the library, of my store, and a small one of me as a child reading *The Lion, The Witch, and the Wardrobe*, still my favorite book. It was lovely and very easy to use to donate, to sign up as a volunteer, or to schedule tutoring for yourself or a child.

As I closed my laptop, I looked around my store, where all the people I loved most in the world were bustling to keep my shop looking nice, answering questions about the program, making book recommendations, and generally throwing themselves into something that would help our community in immeasurable ways. If I hadn't felt so overwhelmed with joy, I might have cried.

Instead, I headed into the children's section to choose books for the new story time we were starting today. The hour for children and their parents had been on the schedule for a few weeks, and I knew we'd have a good turnout. Despite the fact that it meant our busy day was even busier, I was glad people could see and hear about the program when they came in with their children.

Given the ages of the children who I saw wandering the store, I decided on one board book, Sandra Boynton's *Belly Button Book*, and one picture book, an edition of *Rapunzel* with gorgeous illustrations by Paul O. Zelinsky. Between Boynton's word play and Zelinsky's images, I hoped there'd be something to entertain everyone, even the parents.

Fortunately, story time went off without a hitch, and the three dozen children there all browsed with their parents afterwards and gave our already good sales day even more of a boost. One little girl picked up all of Beverly Cleary's Ramona books, and I grinned. I had loved Ramona as a kid.

As the children and their parents headed out, I shook off the fatigue that threatened to settle after I had exerted so much energy entertaining the youngest among us and turned my mind to tonight's event. Mom had been faithfully signing up volunteers and Lu, clients, all morning, and I'd seen more than one parent pick up literature about the fundraiser tonight. I was beginning to get the feeling that it would all come together just fine.

Then, Lucy walked in, and I thought my heart might drop out through the bottom of my ribcage. She didn't try to play off her entrance as casual, but she also didn't beeline toward me where I stood straightening Laura Lippman's books in anticipation of the author's arrival. I sort of froze when I saw her, and then I looked around frantically for someone else who noticed her arrival. Fortunately, Mart had spotted her two and was headed toward us as Lucy and I stared at one another near the front of the store.

As far as I knew, Lucy had been in hiding for almost a week now, and I couldn't figure out for the life of me why she was here now. If she wanted to turn herself in, why hadn't she gone to the police station? Or did she not know Tuck was looking for her? Surely running away from the scene when you had tried to destroy evidence was a fairly obvious reason the police might be wanting to talk to you.

The standoff lasted only a few more seconds because Mart grabbed my arm and dragged me forward toward the young woman. Mart's intervention was fortunate because I was a half second away from shouting, "What are you doing here?," which would have been a mistake given the crowd in the shop just then.

Instead, as we approached, I said calmly and miraculously, "Hi Lucy. Good to see you. How can I help?"

Mart gawked at me, at my calmness, I presume, and I had to admit I was a bit amazed at myself, too, given that I wanted to grab this woman and shake her. But my softer words seemed to calm Lucy a bit, and she stepped forward. "I'm sorry, Harvey," she whispered. "I shouldn't have run."

I rocked back on my heels at her words and the sincerity with which they were spoken. I instinctively wanted to believe her, and while my instincts were typically right, I knew better than to trust them completely, especially today when my mind and emotions were running hot. "Why did you then?" I asked.

"I was scared," she said.

I let out a long breath. "Scared of?"

She glanced around. "No one could know."

"About the note?" Mart asked.

Lucy nodded.

Out of the corner of my eye, I saw a customer waiting to talk to me, so I reached out and took Lucy's arm. "Can you wait for me in the café?"

"I'll sit with you, Lucy," Mart said and took the young woman's arm to lead her away.

I talked with the customer for a few minutes and appreciated the time recommending some of my favorite essayists, including Sloane Crosley and Gretel Ehrlich, so that I could pull myself together a bit. Talking about pieces of literature that had taught me and stilled me always helped, and essays often did that better than any other type of writing, at least for me.

By the time, I had rung up the woman's purchases and walked to the café, Lucy was actually smiling. I pulled up a third chair and sat down. I wanted to be casual and ask what was so funny, but I knew that would feel false to everyone, not just me. So I simply waited until Lucy turned to me.

"I am sorry, Harvey," Lucy said again.

I nodded. "I hear you, but sorry for what, Lucy?" Then I put my hand on hers. "Wait, don't tell me anything that I might need to repeat to the sheriff."

Her eyes grew wide. "What do you mean? I shouldn't have thrown the note away, I know, but would that get me arrested?"

I sighed. "No, probably not, although it was destroying evidence." I glanced at Mart.

"Lucy, we are worried that you are about to tell us you killed Sidney," Mart said matter-of-factly.

Lucy's hand flew to her mouth, and she let out a tiny squeak as she shook her head violently. "No, no, I didn't. He was trying to help me." She hid her face behind her hands and started to cry.

Mart and I looked at each other and, at the same moment, leaned over and hugged Lucy. "It's okay," Mart said. "You're not alone."

The number of times Mart or my other friends had said those words to me over the years was countless, but every time, the assurance of companionship was what I needed most. Even now, though Mart had spoken to Lucy, I took comfort in knowing that was true for me as well.

I gently pulled one of Lucy's hands down and looked her in the eye. "Are you in trouble?"

Lucy stared at me and then nodded. "I don't know how I got here."

Mart and I scooted our chairs closed.

"I thought I was making my own choice, deciding what was best for me, but now I realize I was bribed and manipulated." The tears rolled down her face, but she didn't crumble.

I nodded. I'd been in situations where I thought I was in control and realized, too late, that I wasn't.

"He bought me things. He took care of my apartment. He came to the events I held at the library. We laughed. I didn't even care that he was so much older." She shook her head. "But now I realize that was just all about making him feel good, feeding into his ego about what a man should do."

Mart sighed. We both knew the look of this, the way men we knew had been taught their job was to care for not to partner. The way some men used that "care" as control. It was exhausting.

"But when I realized he wasn't really invested in anything but himself, I tried to break it off. He threatened me, told me he would take my cat, Snickers, and report me for animal abuse." She took a deep breath then lowered the pitch of her voice. "'It's only a small step from there to implying you abuse the children in the library.'"

"He threatened to say you were a pedophile," Mart whispered with as much shock as a whisper could carry.

Lucy nodded.

"Oh, Lucy," I said as I hugged her again. "Will you tell us who it was?" I thought I knew, but I needed to hear her say the name.

The bell over the door rang, and I turned, on instinct, to look at the customer who had come in. I took a deep breath. It was Laura Lippman.

I looked at Mart, who knew Lippman's face from her book jackets, and sighed. "Lucy, I have to go, but Mart will stay with you and keep talking."

Lucy's face fell, and she stood up. "No, it's okay. I'll be alright. I just needed you to know that I wasn't a bad person."

I stood up with her. "Please, Lucy. Tell Mart who threatened you. We can help." I didn't mention that I hoped Mart could talk her into telling Tuck, but I knew that's just what my best friend would do.

Lucy shook her head. "It's okay. I'm sorry to have bothered you. You obviously have important things to attend to." She gave us a small smile and then walked out the door of the shop.

I groaned. "Poor girl. She might have told us . . ."

Mart nodded. "And we might have confirmed who killed Sidney." She glanced over at Lippman who was smiling near the display of her books. "You go. I'll get a hold of Tuck and update him."

I threw my head back and exhaled loudly. "Okay. Thanks, Mart. See you soon."

As I headed toward the shop floor, Rocky intercepted me with two to-go mugs. "For you and Ms. Lippman." Rocky patted my shoulder and turned back to her counter. That woman was so kind and so perceptive.

I greeted Laura with all the enthusiasm I could muster. I was thrilled she was here – more than thrilled, actually – but Lucy's revelation and the events of the week were wearing me a bit thin. I hoped our guest reader couldn't see that in my face.

If she could, she didn't show it as she gushed over the display and told me how glad she was to be here. "If you don't need me here today," she said, "and don't mind me going to your place without you – since I'm sure you're needed here – I'll just go rest up for tonight."

I smiled and looked over at Marcus and then Mom. They had things under control for a few minutes. "I would love to show you the library where the event will be and then take you to our house. That is, if you fancy a short walk now."

I was eager to spend a little time with our guest and to be a good host, and I knew Henri and Bear would be great companions for her later.

Fortunately, Laura grinned and said, "That's perfect. I might just explore a bit before the reading, that is if you don't mind seeing that my copy of my book for the reading and my signing pen make it to the library later. I don't really want to carry them around." She held out a copy of *My Life as a Villainess,* her new essay collection, that was chock-full of hot pink tabs, and then slid a Uniball Vision Elite pen into the front cover.

"Of course." Marcus had joined us, and after I introduced him, I asked if he'd take special care to be sure Ms. Lippman's things arrived at the event tonight.

"I'd be honored," he said and grabbed an All Booked Up tote off the rack by the register and slid the book inside. It was a good touch, and I loved the possibility that Laura Lippman might carry the name of my store to events with her.

After being sure that our special guest didn't mind some canine company – and regretting that I hadn't asked about pet allergies before agreeing to let her stay at my house – the four of us headed out. We chatted about the town and about books as we walked around the store and back to the library and then took the easiest way to my house. Our conversation was fun and light, and I found myself relaxing for the first time that day.

By the time I unlocked our front door, I was laughing at a story Laura told me about a book signing where someone had come with every book she'd ever written to have her sign. "It was flattering, but man did my hand hurt after," she said.

I assured her that we had a two-book maximum for tomorrow's signing and then gave her a quick tour of the house, including an introduction to Aslan, before handing her the spare key and telling her to make herself at home.

From the way she settled into our comfy couch, I felt confident she would do just that.

11

Mayhem, Taco, and I didn't dawdle on our way back to the store, but we didn't exactly sprint either. The afternoon was sunny with a cool breeze, and I needed a few minutes of extra time to wrap my mind around what Lucy had said as well as to prepare for tonight.

I had to make a very concerted effort to slow down my brain, so I replayed the conversation with Lucy. No matter how I tried to keep her in mind as a suspect in Sidney's murder, I just couldn't do it. Her story rang so true for me, even if I'd never been manipulated into a relationship with an older man. I had been in all sorts of relationships with men who thought their primary job was to tend to me, rather than support me as a person, and I understood exactly what Lucy had experienced. Heck, I could have experienced it myself as a young woman but for the grace . . . I didn't let my mind linger there too long. It was too painful.

The one thing I couldn't figure out was whether Lucy thought this man was capable of killing Sidney. I had been so worried about her as she explained her situation that I hadn't thought to ask that question, but now that I thought about it, I wondered. Had she been laying low because she was afraid she'd be next or just because she didn't want to run into this man?

I realized as I walked that I had been picturing Reeves the whole time we were talking, and he was the most likely candidate, of course. He'd been at the library, he clearly was upset about the fact that Cagle had seen him, and he was, as evidenced by his behavior, a bully. I sighed. But I couldn't go around accusing him of threatening and emotionally abusing Lucy – much less targeting him as the killer – without some proof.

And finding proof wasn't my job, I reminded myself. I could leave that to Tuck and decided to focus on the event tonight and let our very capable sheriff do his job. I would, however, ask Mart what he had said as soon as I saw her.

Taco and Mayhem burst into the store and joined the calm but busy space with gusto by visiting all of our friends, who had assembled near the front to pack supplies and prep for tonight's reading. Then the dogs went to sleep in the fiction section while the rest of us continued to work. We had a few more boxes of books to load into the back of Woody's van. Elle was helping Rocky carry out coffee carafes and boxes of her mom's famous cinnamon rolls. Marcus had already packed my laptop with the sales software loaded, and now he was making sure we had pens and paper, our phone-based credit card swipe, and of course Lippman's book and pen.

I spent the next hour tidying up the store and prepping Laura's signing space for the next morning. I expected we'd have a crowd waiting to see her when we opened for her event, and I didn't want to keep people outside longer than necessary as I set up the table and such.

By five p.m., the store was ready to be closed up early, and I

hung the "Find Us at The Library" sign that Marcus had made
to let anyone who didn't get the notice about our event that
they could still buy books or order them over at our table. I
wasn't going to have any stock besides Lippman's books, but I
would have our inventory and could ring up purchases to be
picked up at the store the next morning.

With everything loaded into Mom and Dad's car and
Woody's van, I told everyone that I'd meet them there and
wanted to give Taco and Mayhem one more walk before they
got tied to a table for the evening. Mart decided to walk with
me, and I appreciated the company almost as much as I loved
the chance to ask her about what Tuck had said.

We kept our pace steady but slow as she filled me in on her
conversation with the sheriff. He had, of course, been eager to
hear about Lucy's information and wanted to talk with her
himself, something that Mart promised we would encourage
her to do as soon as we saw her again. "I told him she was very
scared and suggested that maybe she needed protective
custody, and he agreed," Mart said. "But of course, until he
knows where she is, he can't give her that."

I sighed. "Right. What do you think the odds are that we'll
see her tonight?"

Mart shrugged. "She came to the store today and didn't
seem too anxious about being there. If she loves the library as
much as I think she does, I expect there's a good chance she'll
be around."

I nodded, and part of me hoped so. Part of me, though, was
optimistic that we might get through tonight without any more
drama or surprises. I didn't put much stock in that hope,
though. It never did seem to work out that way.

As we walked up to the library, I forgot all about everything
else, though, because the scene was wonderful. Most of the
food trucks were already in place, and the smell was heavenly
as they prepped for the crowd who would begin to arrive in a

half-hour. The banners along the road looked marvelous and gave people not only a clear picture of where they were to go and park but also advertised the excitement in a fun way.

I waved to Stephen and Walter, who were preparing their small group of Boy Scouts with directions on parking the vehicles after they greeted folks and collected any donations they wanted to give. For a brief moment, I wondered if they'd brought Joe Cagle with them, but when I didn't see him nearby, I assumed he had made the wise choice to stay out of sight lest Reeves come by.

My mind quickly flitted back away from the murder, though, when I saw the way Dad had decorated the stage at the end of the long parking lot where the food trucks were set up. He'd had a huge balloon arch brought in, and it coordinated with the sort of blueish tones on many of Lippman's books. He'd also had poster-size reproductions of many of her book covers made, and they hung like bunting from the front of the stage. He'd put a lovely arm chair from their living room on the platform, and a small table (one I recognized from their guest room) sat beside it with a wine glass and a bottle of sparkling water. A lovely braided rug sat under the chair and table, and it looked like a living room set against the backdrop of the trees and the river behind it. It was gorgeous.

The high school choir director had also been kind enough to loan us his sound system, so I could see Pickle and Bear getting that all arranged for tonight. A microphone on a boom bent low over the chair so Laura could sit and read, but they'd also set up a small music stand off to the side if she wanted to stand and also for us to use for our announcements. Everything for Laura's part of the evening seemed to be in good shape.

I turned my attention to our bookstore table and was thrilled to see that Marcus had already begun his magic with the books. A navy blue table cloth draped to the ground with the banner I'd had made at a local printers hanging from the front. Everyone would know we were All Booked Up as they wandered from truck to truck. Two chairs sat behind the table, and the laptop was open and ready to go. Someone had even managed to secure us one of the coveted extension cord plugs in case we needed to charge the computer.

I began scouting around for the ideal place to leash the dogs so that they wouldn't bark for being too far away but also wouldn't trip everyone walking by. I thought maybe the grass median just beside the table would work and was just heading inside to find something to secure them when Woody came over with a leash spike and held it up. "Your dad gave me this for the dogs. Where do you want it?"

I sighed. My parents had thought of everything, and I smiled as I pointed to the middle of the median and watched Woody screw the spike into the ground. "Good to go," he said before heading over to help Dad secure the wheelchair ramp to the stage just in case any of our guests in wheelchairs or with mobility issues needed to get up there.

With the dogs secured and a few minutes to go before six, I looked for Lu and was pleased to see her truck in a prime spot near the stage. She deserved to have an incredible sales night what with all this work she'd put in. "You all ready?" I asked as I looked up into the window on the side of her truck.

"Ready as I'll ever be. I made triple what I usually do for a day, and I hope it lasts." She wiped the back of her hand across her forehead.

"How did you have time to do that when you were at the store all day?" I asked.

"Well, sleep is a luxury this weekend, but I also had my secret weapon." She reached over into one end of the truck and dragged a small, older woman with silver and black hair out to see me. "This is Tia Juanita, the woman who taught me everything I know about food."

I grinned. "It's nice to meet you Tia Juanita. Your niece is a good student."

Juanita smiled and said, "Gracias. Now, let me hide." She ducked back into the end of the truck where the stove was, and I heard the sizzle of something delicious frying up.

Lu smiled. "She's been cooking all day, and she's a force." My friend looked down. "I couldn't have done this without her."

"I imagine not. Thank you, Tia Juanita," I said to the once-again-hidden woman and waved to Lu as I headed on around to make my plan for what I was going to eat that night.

I stopped at each truck and thanked everyone for being there, and at the "Sweet Thai" truck, I got my first dish of the evening, spring rolls. When I sat down at our bookstore table, I offered one to Marcus, who gladly accepted. We savored our delicious, fresh snack and then helped Rocky and Elle get the last of their free coffee and fifty-cent cinnamon roll plans in place. Rocky didn't want to compete with the gourmet coffee truck, so she'd kept it very simple – free black coffee with cream and sugar. And all the proceeds from the sale of the rolls was going to the Literacy Program.

While Marcus and I helped Elle arrange the last of the sugar packets, Rocky headed over to the "Charging Station" food truck and introduced herself to the fellow baristas. She wanted to be sure they knew she was sending people their way for anything that required froth or steam, and, as she said when she came back, "They make a cinnamon latte that is amazing." She held up her cup and let me smell.

I made a quick note to be sure to end the night with a decaf one of those. It smelled heavenly.

For the last five minutes before the crowds arrived, I rushed around with Elle and helped her put out flowers, first on the stage and then around the library and finally on the picnic tables Mom had recruited from the local park. She dropped off the final bouquet at my table before announcing she needed a burger from "Ground Heaven" and wandering into the growing crowd.

The next time I looked up, the entire parking lot was full, and people were milling around the various tables that had been set around in the close-cut lawn. Two children were playing with Taco and Mayhem, who were delighted to have the attention and give up their bellies for pats.

We'd have a steady stream of customers who wanted to buy Lippman's books plus a few other special orders. People were eager to get their number for the signing event in the morning. The number system was something Marcus suggested just as the gates opened, and I'm glad he had presumed I'd agree because it was clear that if we didn't have some sort of system, the store was going to be a truly wild place in the morning.

A half-hour into the event, we'd already given out seventy-five numbers from the roll Marcus had convinced the deli counter at the local grocery store to give him as their token of support for the event. I had a feeling we would be well into the five hundreds before the night was over, and I was very glad we'd set up the special order system because we were going to run out of books long before the customers thinned.

I glanced over toward Mom's table, where she was busily telling people about the literacy program and signing up folks to volunteer and, it looked like, for tutoring too. When two fathers walked by with their young son, I heard one of the men say, "This feels like a real gift just when we needed one, doesn't it?" His partner looked at him and smiled. "The same day his teacher said he needed help with reading." I smiled as they glanced at me, clear I had overheard and seemingly glad I had.

"If your son ever wants to come by the store, we have some great books that will tie in with the tutoring program, gifts for those learning to love to read," I said as they came closer. I handed them a card with the information about our new monthly book giveaway and story time and told them I looked forward to seeing them soon. The little boy smiled at me as he ran his fingers over the covers of the books. He was already a book-lover, I could see it, and I was so glad we had a way to help him be a reading lover, too.

I had been reading since before I went to school, thanks to my parents' love of books and their willingness to read me anything and everything, but I had friends of all ages who struggled with reading. Sometimes it was simply that they'd never found the books they loved, and sometimes it was something more challenging than a good recommendations like ADD or ADHD or dyslexia. The program Mom had set up in my honor was going to train the tutors in all those things, from finding books the readers adored to helping them with accommodations that they could use their whole reading lives. Seeing that little boy and hearing how he was going to get some help to do what I most loved gave me a real thrill.

I didn't have much time to settle into that excitement though because our sales were fast and steady, and Marcus and I kept busy unpacking more boxes of books, ordering additional titles by Lippman and others, and giving out numbers for the signing. Before I knew it, almost an hour had passed and Laura was waving as she headed toward the stage. I was glad she'd wisely avoided the crowd around the table because I wanted her to save her energy for the reading, and I didn't want any overenthusiastic fans to bombard her with autograph requests right then.

Earlier as we'd walked to my house, we'd agreed that she would bring a change of clothes and a baseball cap with her so that she could scoot inside, change, and then browse with a little anonymity. Henri and Bear were going to continue to be her guides for the evening, and I had a feeling that they would make a big enough show of Lippman leaving that no one would suspect her as she wandered the food trucks that she had said she absolutely didn't want to miss.

Now, Mom greeted her and helped her settle into a chair by the side of the stage before waving me over. I had agreed to do the welcome, and nothing more, but I was going to be first up for the mic. I stood and told Marcus I'd see him in a minute before taking deep breaths as I walked up to the stage, said a quick hello to Laura, and gave Mom a quick hug. Then, it was seven and time to get started.

"Thank you all for coming," I began as I went on to thank everyone for attending, tell them that they'd learn more about the Literacy Program they were supporting tonight, and remind them that we had just a few copies of Lippman's books that would be for sale *after* her reading. "I don't want any of you missing a word she says," I said to a small chuckle through the crowd. "Now, let me introduce my one and only Mama, the woman who made this all happen."

Mom leapt onto the stage with the enthusiasm of a young girl and headed toward the mic. I listened to her describe the program to everyone gathered, cajole them to sign up as volunteers or to get tutoring, and thank Laura for coming.

I was just settling back into my seat at the table and about to take a bite of the amazing grilled cheese sandwich from "Cheesing It Up" that I'd asked Marcus to grab for me when my mom's voice grew softer in tone. "Now, I want to just tell you a little bit about the amazing woman this program is named after. You just met her, in fact, my daughter, Harvey Beckett." She waved an arm in my direction, and I set my sandwich back down.

"My daughter is a fierce woman, not in an angry or violent sense, but in the sense that she fights for what she believes is right. She had to fight hard to open her bookstore, All Booked Up, here in this gorgeous town, and she's chosen to fight for people and justice her whole life. She loves words more than any other – inanimate!" she raised a finger to emphasize that point, "thing on the earth, so we could not name this program after a better person. Join me in thanking Harvey."

The crowd cheered and clapped, and I saw Laura give me a big thumbs up even as she climbed the stage to join Mom, who gave her a stupendous and well-deserved introduction.

For the next forty minutes, the crowd grew reasonably quiet as Laura read her well-marked copy of her latest book and then talked a bit about what reading and writing had meant in her life and throwing her enthusiastic support behind the literacy program. She finished her time on the stage by taking questions, which Pickle helped facilitate with a wireless mic that he circulated amongst the crowd. Laura's answers were honest and often funny, and people seemed to be really enjoying her time.

Before she left the stage, she did us one last kindness and announced that there was also a small memorial area dedicated to long-time library director, Sidney Scott, inside. She encouraged people to go see the art made in his honor and to visit the tutoring room that was now named for him. She also gave a good plug for the book sale, which was a lovely gift since it encouraged even the out-of-town folks to take a stroll through the building.

Then, before I knew it, she was done, and I saw Henri meet her at the edge of the stage and direct her to their car, which pulled out of the library parking lot and headed South. They would double around to the back door, where Mindy was going to meet them and let them in so Laura could change. And given the way that people had watched her go and then moved back into the space to get more food and visit us, I felt sure that no one suspected she would return.

Still, when I saw her Henri come back with a woman in an Orioles cap, my heart sped up just a bit. But no one else paid them any mind, and I put my attention back on selling books and then taking orders with the promise that Laura would return later in the year to sign them since we had already given out our cache of numbers for the next morning's signing.

AN HOUR AND A HALF LATER, the crowd had almost entirely dispersed, Laura had eaten two of Lu's tacos as well as at least one of Lucas's cupcakes, which had been very popular. They'd had so many customers that Cate had stayed with him all night to help sell instead of circulating herself as planned. Now, Mart was escorting Laura home as Stephen, Walter, Woody, and the rest of us cleaned up.

I felt a little disappointed that I hadn't been able to make it around to more of the vendors, especially the "Fry Guys" truck that specialized in Belgian frites, but the night had been more of a success than we could have imagined with well over fifteen-hundred people in attendance. Marcus and I had sold out of books by eight-thirty, and our special orders stack was a half-inch think . We'd capped the signing numbers at five hundred, and I knew we'd be pushing it to be able to fit all those people in the store at once. We would do it though, somehow. We always did.

Once everything was packed up and the crowd gone, Mom ushered me to the single table left in the middle of the parking lot, and soon the vendors were bringing over their remaining dishes for all of us workers to eat. Rocky even talked to her fellow baristas and had them bring me a decaf cinnamon latte.

We all stood around eating and talking, celebrating together, and I was delighted to see vendors sharing business cards and to hear about the events they were recommending to each other. I knew that tonight had likely been a financial success of some sort for all of them, even with their donations to the literacy program, but as a small business owner myself, I really wanted this to be a springboard to future success, too.

Thankfully, Galen had spent the night capturing photos of

each vendor and tagging them on his Instagram feed with notes about where the trucks would be the following day, and the Halal gyro vendor laughed with delight when Laura tagged him in her FB post with the line – "Best Gyro Ever!"

Just as the trucks began to close up for the night, Mindy joined us, and I was glad Luke had thought to save her a cupcake because she looked beat. "How did the dedication of Sidney's room and the art in his honor go?" I asked. I hadn't been able to break away to go in, but I was hoping it had been well attended.

"We had a good crowd, thanks to all of you telling people about it, and the book sale was a huge success too." She smiled. "We sold over seven hundred dollars' worth of books and pretty much cleared out our surplus of titles."

Mom grinned. "That's great. I'm so glad."

"And," a woman's voice said from behind me, "We got about fifty people library cards, so that's a win, too." I turned to see Lucy smiling.

Tuck walked across the lot from the library and shook Lucy's hand. "That is good news," he said. "And we had no security incidents tonight, so that is a relief."

I smiled and was glad to see that, clearly, Lucy had talked to Tuck. The air wouldn't be this free of tension if she hadn't. Tuck was professional, but he would have asked to talk to Lucy immediately if he hadn't already done so.

There were too many people around to talk about their discussion just then, though, so I didn't ask. Instead, I gathered Lucy in a hug and whispered, "You okay?"

She nodded. "I am," she whispered. "I'm staying with Tuck and Lu for a few nights."

I sighed. "Good. I was worried," I said. "And your mom?"

"On her annual cruise to the Caribbean," Lucy said. "It's nice for her and a chance for me to get to know new friends."

"She's in good hands, Harvey," Lu said as she joined us.

"Ready to ride? Tia Juanita is eager to see you drive this thing." She pointed over her head toward the food truck.

Lucy laughed. "Bring it on," she said.

Marcus and Dad had already taken our cardboard boxes back to the recycling dumpster, and Mindy had arranged for the library's trash service to do an extra run for all the trash from the night. With the food trucks caravanning out and my friends waving and heading home, all that was left was to get the dogs and hitch a cozy ride home with Taco and Mayhem in the back seat of Mom and Dad's car.

We all loaded up, and as soon as everyone was in a car and those cars were started, the line of vehicles began to move out. Dad, as always, waited to be sure everyone was on their way before pulling out himself. It was a small kindness I'd always admired him for.

I sank back into my seat and gazed at the almost empty parking lot and field that had been so full just hours before. That's when I saw it, the flutter of movement at the edge of the trees behind the stage. Someone was there, and they were watching us.

12

I spent the short ride to my house trying to convince myself that I had just been imagining things, but by the time Dad pulled up to my house, I knew I needed to let Tuck in on what I'd seen.

After I waved goodbye to Mom and Dad at the door and before I went inside, I shot off a quick text to Tuck and then slid my phone into my back pocket. I didn't need to be involved any further, and I wanted to give our special guest my full attention.

Inside, Mart, Symeon, and Laura were at the kitchen island with glasses of wine and a bowl of trail mix. I grinned. This was my kind of after party.

Taco and Mayhem greeted our visitor briefly and then took to their beds by the fireplace to sleep off their people hangover. I was glad because as gracious as Laura was with their sniffing, she didn't seem the kind of person who really enjoyed dog kisses or cuddles in the kind of plentitude my pooches could give.

We stayed up late talking about books and good food, about Laura's writing process and her plans for the next few years. She was inspiring as she looked at the years when many considered retiring as an opportunity to keep doing the work she loved and giving us readers, her fans, many more books to look forward to. I hoped I felt the same way about the bookstore in twenty years.

About midnight, though, the events of the week and the excitement of the night caught up to me, and fatigue plowed into my arms and legs so forcefully that I thought I might just curl up on the kitchen floor to sleep. When I yawned for the third time, Laura stood and said she was going to head to her room and hit the sack, and I was grateful for her courtesy and for the fact that she didn't take my fatigue personally.

We hadn't told her about the murder because we didn't want to make the crime writer think we were asking for her sleuthing skills to be put to work and because we didn't want to worry her, although I didn't think she was the type to really worry about that kind of thing. She might hear something in the morning, but I expected she'd be too busy signing to do much chit-chat. That seemed like a good thing in all cases.

DESPITE THE FACT that Aslan took full advantage of the fact that the dogs were too tired to move from their living room beds and slept between my legs all night, I rested well, and when my alarm went off at eight, I woke without the desire to snooze even once. We had a big day ahead, my favorite kind of day, a book lovers' day.

I showered and headed into the living room, glad to see everyone else was still resting, including the pups. I let the dogs out for their morning business and then filled the three food bowls, Aslan's on top of the fridge where Taco's greedy mouth couldn't reach it, although he did try.

Then, I quietly poured myself a bowl of cereal and drank my coffee while I enjoyed the golden spring sun outside, wrote Symeon a thank you note for managing breakfast, and then wrote another to Laura and Mart to tell them I'd see them at the store. They knew our plan was to do the signing at ten-fifteen, and I'd suggested Laura either come about nine-thirty so she could get inside and settled comfortably in a quiet corner until the signing or that she come right after ten so she could go right to the signing table. She'd intimated that she wanted to come in early, so I looked forward to quiet time with her then.

Home business taken care of, I leashed up the dogs and made the walk into town. Along the way, my neighbors' peonies were just beginning to open, and I admired the way Spring created a succession of show that kept the color going for weeks. I quickened my step as I remembered that Elle was going to bring a new batch of flowers for the store this morning. I loved new flower day almost as much as new book day. It was always a burst of colorful surprise, and I hoped this morning she might have some peony blossoms for us.

I had thought maybe I'd beat Marcus and Rocky in this morning, but of course I was wrong. The lights were on, and when I unlocked the door and walked in, I could smell the perfume of coffee wafting through the air. "You two get the prize for hardest workers!" I shouted into the shop.

From the kitchen of the café, Rocky said, "Well, we didn't have a world-famous author at our houses."

"And I live two minutes down the street," Marcus added as he came from the back room with a stack of books. Marcus continued to rent an apartment over the mechanic's garage in town, even though the mechanic had moved closer to Baltimore for a new job. It was a great deal for him, low rent and close to work, but I knew the owner, Daniel, also appreciated having someone in the building.

Because of the crowd we were expecting today, all of us wanted to have the store in great shape and to have as many things done early as possible. So we scurried around straight-

ening and filling the shelves while Rocky filled an entire shelf
of her pastry case with her mother's cinnamon rolls. Her mom
must have baked all week.

I was really hoping today would be banner sales day for all
of us. Anything the bookstore made in income today was bonus
because last night, just from the sales of Lippman's books and
special orders at the fundraiser, we had already made our sales
goal for the weekend. But I was hoping to be able to donate a
large (at least large for me) sum to the literacy program at the
end of the weekend, so any sales today would help me be able
to do that with gusto.

Just at nine, Elle came in with two five-gallon buckets full of
flowers, and she set about filling all the vases in the café and
then came to the register with a towel and created an amazing
arrangement of peonies, irises, and fresh rosemary and basil.
By the time she was done, the entire store smelled like a spring
meadow and a great dinner all at one time, and somehow, even
the undertones of coffee from the café mixed in well. I took a
deep breath, looked at my friend and said, "Wow. You are really
good at this."

Elle laughed. "I hope so. It is my livelihood, after all." She
took a few extra vases from beneath the register and added a
few springs of basil and a single flower to them before scat-
tering them around the store. Then, she set a special arrangement of just the herbs on the signing table. "The floral scents
give some people the sneezes or headaches, and if this bothers
Lippman, just move it okay?" Elle said to me.

I nodded as the bell over the door rang and Laura and Mart
came in. Mart turned and relocked the door behind her, and
then she smiled. "It smells amazing in here," she said.

Laura nodded. "Agreed," she said as she turned to Elle who
had her buckets with a few remaining stems in hand. "You're
responsible for this?"

Elle blushed. "I am. It's nice to meet you, Ms. Lippman. I

was just telling Harvey that if anything bothers you, to just remove it."

"Bothers me? Nope, not at all. But I appreciate the thoughtfulness." She smiled again and then looked at the display of her books that Marcus was just finishing up. "That looks so good," she said.

Marcus beamed. "Thank you." He turned to her. "I hope we have enough copies of everything."

"Me, too," I said. "We've sold a lot of our stock in the past few days, and last night had big sales, too. Sorry we don't have more copies."

Laura looked at the stacks of books. "Are you serious, Harvey? You have dozens of my books, and you've already sold dozens. I've been to signings where the manager only got twenty copies, and we sold out in five minutes. This is great."

I took a deep breath of relief and realized I had been more nervous than I thought about all of this. I was glad she was happy, and I was glad she'd come early so that she could enjoy the store before the crowd came in.

"Mind if I take a look around?" she said.

"Not at all. Would you like a tour, or would you prefer to just wander?" I asked.

"Let me just wander. That way, I can have the joy of discovery, and you can have a little time to catch your breath." She meandered off into the fiction section, and I smiled. Laura Lippman was browsing in *my* bookstore.

As Elle headed out the door, Cate and Lucas came in, and I smiled as I glanced the small group of people who were already milling by the door. "We'll be open in about twenty minutes," I said before I locked the door again.

"We're here to help," Cate said. "Put us to work."

I smiled. "Cate, would you mind being Laura's assistant? Open the books to the title page and keep people moving if they get too chatty."

"You got it." She moved to the signing table.

"And me?" Lucas asked.

"Feel like being on line patrol?" I asked. "Check numbers to be sure we are, roughly, honoring the order we promised. Be sure people have paid for their books before they get them signed. Remind people that there's a two-book maximum for signing. Keep people happy as they wait."

"On it," he said. "If you want to give me your keys, I'll also staff the door, talk up the crowd outside, and be in charge of opening her up whenever you say go."

I tossed him my keys. "Perfect." I took a deep breath. Their help was going to mean that Marcus and I could staff the register and help customers in general.

As Lucas went out to work the growing crowd, Walter, Stephen, Henri and Bear slipped in. "Tell us what to do," Stephen said.

I glanced around for a minute, at a loss for where I needed help but sure I did need it.

"I could use the men over here," Rocky said, and immediately, Bear, Walter, and Stephen headed her way. I chuckled at the idea of those three middle-aged guys bussing tables and slinging lattes, but they were all smiling, eager to help. I really had the best friends.

"Why don't I keep the back end of things going?" Henri said. "Refill your bag supply at the register. Check on the bathrooms. That kind of thing."

"That would be amazing," I said. "I hadn't even thought of that, but yes, that would be a big help."

"Great. Show me where you keep the supplies?" We headed to the back room, and I gave her a quick tour of where we kept things. I wanted to pull down another box of toilet paper, but I had to move a couple of boxes first. They were heavy, book heavy, and when I opened them up to see what had been tucked behind our break table, I found two boxes of Laura's titles.

I jumped up and down a little, and Henri said, "Nice. I'll help you carry them up."

I pulled down the box of toilet paper so Henri could access it easily, and then she and I toted the books to Marcus who smiled when he saw them and quickly fleshed out the display.

Outside the door, the line was already beginning to stretch past the windows, and I could see Lucas chatting with people and checking their signing number as he shifted people into their assigned order. My heart skipped. It was going to be an amazing day.

And it was, for most of the morning. Laura signed and talked casually but not too long, thanks to Cate's gentle nudging of the customers. I staffed the register and rang up books before allowing those customers to get into the back of the line to get Laura's autograph if time allowed. Lucas had people laughing all the way down the queue, and Marcus kept the other customers and the store in general happy. Over in the café, Bear and Stephen were keeping tables clean and open as fast as they could, and Rocky had enlisted Walter to help serve pastries while she steamed milk. I couldn't keep the smile off my face.

That is until I saw Lucy in the line. I was actually very glad to see her, but I felt anxiety tingle up my spine because of how exposed she was. If whoever it was who was controlling her was here, he was bound to see her. Last night, the media had been there, so I hadn't been surprised she had been safe. But here, things were much more low-key. Tuck hadn't even been in yet.

Still, there wasn't much I could do except rip off a text to Tuck and hope he might be available to come by and keep an eye out.

He'd replied to my text about seeing someone at the library the night before with an efficient, "Thanks for letting me know," which left me confused about whether I was bothering him with my observations or if he was just tired and concerned. I decided to think the latter because I didn't want to worry that my friend was upset with me.

His reply to this morning's notice about Lucy was super-quick. "Oh man. Thanks for letting me know, Harvey. We'll be right over."

I took this "Thanks" as sincere and decided the other message was, too. Still, I wasn't about to take any chances and asked Mart if she could take over at the register while I went to check in with customers. She'd been helping Marcus keep the display of Laura's books filled, but she readily took over for me when I tilted my head to where Lucy stood in line. "You let Tuck know?" she asked as she slid in beside me.

I nodded. "He's on his way." I walked casually down the line of customers, speaking to some folks I knew and welcoming those I didn't, until I got to Lucy. I smiled at her and tried to keep my voice light as I said, "You a Lippman fan?"

Lucy's eyes lit up, but she didn't smile. "I am. A big one, and I know this is a risk, Harvey, but I couldn't stay away. She's my favorite author."

I patted her on the shoulder and smiled, very aware of the close proximity of about a quadrillion people. I didn't need to make a scene or get anyone worried. "I'm glad you came, and Tuck is coming too."

Lucy swallowed. "That's great. I didn't think to tell him I was coming here when I saw him at breakfast. Probably should have, huh?"

I nodded and smiled as she kept her tone light. She clearly understood that I was speaking in generalities for a reason, and I was grateful she played along. "Good. You let me know if you need anything?"

"Will do," she said and smiled again.

I moved on down the line behind her, for the sake of

pretense, but I soon found myself caught up in the moment and the way the line for signatures was now snaking around into the café, even as more people came in, swept up Laura's books, and headed to see Mart to make their purchase. The display was beginning to look thin, but I was grateful we'd found those other two boxes since it meant we still had something of hers to sell.

I was just making my way to the end of the line when I saw Tuck and Watson, both in plain clothes, walk in. They waved at some folks they knew and then separated to wander around the store. Tuck was always so good about honoring my business and the need to not alarm my customers, and today I was particularly grateful.

On my way back to the register, I knelt down by Laura to see how she was doing. "Any hand cramps, yet?"

She smiled. "Not yet. This is great, Harvey. Thanks."

"No, thank *you*," I said as I stood. "You let me know if you need a break or want me to call an end to this wonderful madness."

"Will do," she said as she went on to meet the next guest and take his book from Cate.

Before I could relieve Mart, Tuck intercepted me and asked if I had a copy of *Odd Thomas* in the back room because he didn't see it on the shelves. Our sheriff was a big reader, but not of thrillers, especially not thrillers where the main character can see the dead, so I knew something was up and led him to the back room to "help me look." I had just seen the book on the shelves this morning and hadn't rung it up for anyone, so if I had any doubt that Tuck wanted to speak in private, that confirmed it.

As soon as the door closed behind us, Tuck turned to me and said, "We're going to be here all day, Harvey. Lucy still hasn't been willing to tell me who threatened her, but I imagine you know my suspect."

"Reeves," I said without hesitation.

"Exactly. You haven't seen him here today, right?"

"Nope. Not a sign of him."

"Could it have been him you saw last night at the library?"

I thought back at what I'd seen. Definitely a silhouette, and while I couldn't be sure and didn't want to presume, my brain had thought the person was a man. But beyond that, I couldn't say more. "It could have been. I think it was a man, but I didn't see any of his features and couldn't even really tell you how tall he was or anything. He was in the tree line, so it was even darker around him than out where I was."

Tuck nodded. "Okay. If it's alright with you, I'll let everyone we trust know that we're on the look-out, and I'm going to suggest Lucy spend her day at the store. Alright?"

"Sounds good. I'll let you know if I see him. Maybe we need to have a signal, a code word?" I smirked.

Tuck rolled his eyes. "I think, 'He's here' will be sufficient." I was glad to see him smiling when he headed out there, a copy of some random paperback under his arm just to keep his cover story intact.

I headed back to the register and updated Mart on the situation. She took it all in and said, "Some days I wish we had more police officers in this town."

"If they were all like Tuck, I'd be down," Marcus said as he walked up with a stack of magazines for Mart to reshelve.

"Yeah," I said quietly. "We've got some good ones here," I said as I saw Watson open a copy of *The Westing Game* and settle into a chair that had a clear view of the door. I'd have to ask him if that choice was random or if he loved that book as much as I did.

It was already eleven-fifteen, and the line for Laura's autograph, while no longer growing, was still trailing into the cafe. I decided to trust that, as a grown woman, she would let me know if she needed me and went back to ringing up purchases.

I was so busy that I almost missed Lucy's turn at the signing table, but I was glad to catch the joy on her face as Laura greeted her. I saw Cate lean over to Laura and say what I assumed was a little bit more about Lucy because Laura stood up and shook her hand before signing not just two but four books for her. I'd have to ask Cate what she said to prompt that bonus from Laura, especially after a solid hour and a half of small talk and writing the same thing over and over.

When Lucy had gotten her signatures, I saw her stroll over and drop into the chair next to Watson before opening her copy of *Wilde Lake* and beginning to read. Somehow, I didn't think a librarian would much mind being forced to read all day, especially when the book was by her favorite author.

By noon, the signing line was gone, almost every one of our copies of Lippman's books had sold and left with her signature, and I was not only ready for lunch but ready to get off my feet for a few minutes. I offered to get Laura some food, to have something delivered for us to eat in the café, but she said she needed to get on home. I didn't blame her. That much chatting would have been more than my share for a whole week.

She said a kind thank you to everyone who had helped and then headed, with Stephen as her escort, to her car which was in the parking lot next door. I waved as she drove back by the shop on her way out of town, and then I sank into a chair in the café and took a deep breath. We had done it.

I was just beginning to wonder if I should get pizza delivered for everyone when Lu came in with a tray of tamales and another of tacos. "I figured you'd need some food, and so I made a double batch today."

I laughed with delight. "You are amazing, Lu. Let me get you some cash for these," I said as I stood and headed toward the register.

"Don't you dare, Harvey Beckett," she said. "These are my gift to all of you for the work last night. THANK YOU. The vendors were ecstatic, and now I have lots of new contacts for my business. I'm headed to a festival in Annapolis next weekend, in fact."

"That's great news. Will Tia Juanita be joining you? I mean, it seems like you'd need another pair of hands," I asked as I helped myself to two chicken tacos.

"She will, and my niece is coming, too. It's going to be a family business, like I've always dreamed." She said and beamed at her husband who had come up beside her.

"Thanks, love," he said as he kissed her on the cheek. "I'm going to be here today. Any chance you fancy a game of gin rummy?"

Lu laughed. "Sounds perfect. Let me get through the lunch rush, and then I'll close up for the day. Be back in an hour?"

"I'll be waiting," Tuck said as he headed toward the café with some tamales.

I wandered slowly through the store while Marcus staffed the register and invited everyone who had helped for the past two days to come get some food. Lu had brought all the paper products we needed, and so one by one by friends came by the signing table where the food was set up and filled a plate. When they all had their fill, I let the customers know they were welcome to sample Lu's food if they liked. We had only a couple of tamales and a steak taco left, but a teenage boy and his dad scooped those up and then asked where they could find more. I pointed to Lu's truck, which was parked just up the street, and they headed off with a couple more customers trailing behind.

I bought out Rocky's supply of Italian sodas and handed them around to my friends before taking over the register for Marcus so that he could dig into the plate Rocky had fixed for him. I took a deep breath and listened to the murmur of my friends' voices as they laughed and talked, and then I smiled at the customers who were still wandering the floor, especially the two or three who had stacks of books tucked under their arms. I was grateful for the sales, of course, but more than that I just loved seeing people who couldn't resist the lure of books. They were my people almost as much as all those wonderful human beings eating lunch behind me.

As I tucked into my own tacos, I looked for Lucy and found her back in her chair, a tamale on a plate next to her, and Lippman's book wide open. Lucy was my people, too, it seemed. I just wished she'd trust me, or better yet Tuck, with the name of the person she feared. I was learning, finally in my fifth decade, though, that you couldn't make people do what they didn't want to do. We just had to keep showing her that we cared and could be trusted, and she'd tell us when she was ready. At least I hoped so – and I hoped she'd talk before she got hurt.

ABOUT MID-AFTERNOON, my parents stopped by. They'd offered to come in this morning to help, but I knew they both needed rest, more rest than they'd required when they were younger. I also knew they wouldn't take it if I put it like that, so I suggested they stay home, tally the totals from the fundraiser, and come in later today to so that we could let Galen and Mrs. Dawson know. They'd spread the word, and maybe the good results would spur some larger, more long-term donations.

Now, here they were and given the smile on Mom's face as she walked over to me, I knew the figures were good, very good by the looks of it. "So it was a success?"

"More than we hoped for," she said and hanged me a slip of paper that said $12,853.

"Whoa, that's huge, Mom." I looked down at the paper again. "Wow, and that doesn't include my donation yet."

"You don't have to do—"

I interrupted my mom. "I know I don't have to, Mom. I want to, and it's a good business move, too," I said as I caught Dad's eye. "You can start a corporate donor program with me as the founding donor."

Dad laughed. "Now you're thinking like a business woman, Harvey." He glanced around at the store. "Actually, you are a business woman, a good one. I like how you're thinking ahead, though."

"If you guys have a few minutes, I can run my numbers from last night and this morning and get you a check right now." I was eager to see our totals anyway, but I also liked that my store's name would be in the initial announcement of the results.

"Sure," Mom said. "I could use a little mid-afternoon treat anyway. Think Rocky has anymore cinnamon rolls?"

"I doubt it given the crowd this morning, but she does sometimes have a secret stash." I stepped over to the register, scanned to be sure no customers were headed my way, and shifted the computer to reporting mode.

I had just printed out our totals, stifled a squeal of glee for the sake of good taste, and written out my check for two thousand dollars when Reeves walked into the shop.

Tuck had been sitting in the café reading, but now he was striding toward Reeves with Watson close behind him. I was closer, though, and for the sake of my other customers, I picked up my pace so I could greet the man first. "Can I help you with something, Mr. Reeves?"

He scowled at me and looked a bit puzzled. "I'm looking for the sheriff. The woman at the station said I could find him here."

Tuck closed the last few steps and said, "What can I do for you, Reeves?" Tuck spread his feet wide and put his hands on his hips, and I was reminded of the advice hikers were given about black bears. "Make yourself look as big as possible."

I took a deep breath, caught Watson's eye, and when I saw his nod, I walked away as casually as I could all the while scanning the room for Lucy. I found her a moment later, now tucked into the quieter corner of the history section, her book close to her face as her eyes zoomed across the last few pages. She was a fast reader, and I loved that.

I hated to interrupt her, but she needed to know Reeves was here. "Lucy, I'm sorry," I said as I put my hand on her knee.

She squeaked and squished back against the chair a bit before meeting my eyes and visibly relaxing. "Sorry, Harvey. You surprised me."

"I get that way at the end of a book, too. I should have said something as I walked over. So sorry." I got a bit closer and knelt by her chair. "Lucy, Reeves is here."

A small line formed between her eyebrows. "Is that someone you want me to meet or something?"

I studied her face, and it was clear she had no idea who I was talking about. "You don't know him?"

She shook her head. "No. Should I?"

"No, don't worry about it. I just made a mistake and thought he was someone you knew. Go back to your work."

She looked at me carefully for a minute as if she wanted to say something, but then she sighed and said, "Thanks" before scanning for her place on the page and dropping back into the story.

Clearly, Reeves was not the man who had threatened Lucy. Good book or no, no one who felt afraid could slide back into a book that easily, not even the most avid reader.

As I reached the counter again, I could see Tuck and Reeves with their heads bent low over the table between them. Tuck was frowning, but I didn't see any anger or frustration in his expression. Instead, it looked like whatever Reeves was telling Tuck had him worried. I wondered what that was all about.

Watson was nearby, still with a book open in front of him, but I could tell he was paying close attention to his boss as well as keeping an eye on the store. Something was up, and it had both of these police officers concerned.

The rest of my friends had left after lunch, and so I needed to ask for Mom and Dad's help. I made a show of walking over with the check from the store in my hands, and I spoke a little too loudly when I handed it to Mom. She gave me a puzzled look, and I just smiled brighter as I tilted my head toward the table where Tuck and Reeves sat.

Dad followed my hint and saw the men talking. "Harvey, could you recommend a new biography for me?" he asked as he stood up.

Mom looked from me to him but then played right along. "Your dad is plowing through books these days," she said as she stood too. "Thank you for this, too, Harvey. I'll get in touch with Galen and Mrs. Dawson now and let them know they can make the announcement."

"And I'll let Laura know. I think she'll be thrilled," I said as we walked toward the biography section at the back of the store. As soon as we were behind a tall shelf of spirituality books, I said, "Dad, there's a situation. I don't know exactly what's going on, but can you stay near that blonde woman reading over there?"

I casually glanced at Lucy, who had moved onto another book in her stack, before turning back to Dad. "She's in danger, but I don't know from whom yet."

"Harvey, don't you think the two police officers in the front have this covered?" Mom asked, her concern for Dad's safety obvious in the tremor in her voice.

"I do, which is the only reason I feel comfortable asking Dad to stay near Lucy." I sighed. "I want her to know someone is keeping an eye on her. She needs that reassurance. I'll explain later."

Dad hugged me to him quickly. "You've got it, Harvey. Now, I really do need something to read."

I smiled and pulled a copy of *The Hairstons* by Henry Wiencek off the shelf. "Not a standard bio, but a great story about a family. I think you'll like it."

With a wave of the book, Dad dropped into a chair nearby and turned it slightly so he could keep Lucy in his line of sight. I passed by Lucy's seat and casually pointed out that the man in the chair nearby was my dad before Mom and I walked back to the front. I set her up at a café table to contact Galen and Mrs. Dawson about her amazing fundraising total and so that she was close to the police officers if something went down.

After sending my own text to Laura and getting back her enthusiastic, "That's great." I decided I needed to put the escapades around Lucy out of my mind. Tuck and Reeves were still talking, and Watson was still keeping an eye on the store. With Lucy guarded by an attentive watcher, I knew I had done everything I could and decided to focus on my business for a bit.

Marcus was due to finish his shift in a half-hour, so before he left, we printed out next week's return list and then went around the store to evaluate what we needed to order to fill our shelves and replace the titles we'd sold and those we were going to return to the distributor.

Between that focused work and the customers who kept steadily making purchases, the next thirty minutes flew by, and by the time Marcus headed out for the day, I felt like we were in good shape for the week, especially since the store was quiet and I could place our orders before we closed this evening.

A bit later, Rocky stopped over with a latte and asked if I thought it would disturb anyone if she started to clean up a little early. "I'm kind of dead on my feet, and I'd like to be able to leave as soon as we close."

I smiled. "Of course. And I'll do the same. We should be able to turn off the sign and walk out of here right at seven."

"Perfect," she said as she headed back to her corner of the

store and I continued entering titles into the store's wonderfully large order for next week.

About six, Mom came over and asked if I would mind if she contacted everyone to suggest a potluck at my house for seven-thirty, and I smiled. "That sounds perfect, Mom."

I walked over to let Dad know the plan and when I saw Lucy, I decided to invite her, too. She was a very sweet woman, and since Tuck and Lu would be invited, I figured she might want to come along. Plus, I didn't think it was wise for her to go anywhere, even Tuck and Lu's house, alone. "Join us for dinner at my place?" I asked as I walked over.

She looked up at me, and I watched the fog of an engrossed reader lift from her eyes. "Um, sure, if that's okay with you."

"More than okay. A bunch of us are gathering. It would be nice to have you join us." I looked at the young woman and thought of myself at that age, how I'd been sure I knew what I needed and how to get it and how I'd been so very wrong. "And if you'd like, you can stay with Mart and me until all this blows over."

Lucy's smile got a bit brighter.

I knew it would be a little bit of a busy night what with the need to change the sheets and spruce up the guest room from last night's visitor, but I also knew that Mart would be fine with it.

"Are you sure?" Lucy asked as she slid a finger into the spine of the book to hold her place. "I mean I'm grateful to the Masons for having me, but it would be nice to hang out with girlfriends for a night.

"Absolutely." Then, I decided to get bold. "I cannot promise food as good as Lu's, but we have lavender soap in the bathroom."

"How can I possibly pass that up?" she said with a laugh.

"Good. We close at seven, so you can walk home with me and whoever else wants to join us there." I glanced over at Dad, who was doing his best to look like he was reading. But since his eyes weren't moving, I knew he was listening. "You're invited too, Dad." I said.

Lucy waved at him tentatively, and Dad looked up and smiled before picking up his club chair and bringing it over to sit next to her. I smiled, and as I walked away, I heard my dad do what my dad does so well, make small talk. "So I hear you're a children's librarian. If you had to list the Top Ten children's books of all time, what would you name?"

I chuckled. I hoped Lucy didn't mind being grilled on recommendations, but from the sound of her laughter, it sounded like she didn't mind a bit.

13

Thanks to a little help from Mom, Dad, and Lucy, the store was in perfect order a few minutes before seven, and as soon as the last customer checked out, we turned off the light, set the alarm, and headed out, with Marcus joining us outside.

Mayhem and Taco led the way as the six of us headed toward my house. Reeves had left quietly a while ago, and with my assurance that Lucy was in good hands, Tuck had said he and Watson had to go take care of police business. Both of them looked very stern and very concerned as they left, but they'd also both said they'd come by my house for some good food as soon as they could.

Everyone else was on their way over, too, with their own dishes to contribute although I was disappointed to hear that Lucas had not been able to reup his cupcake supply for the evening. However, the promise of homemade tiramisu was almost a suitable substitute. I would miss that buttercream icing though.

Mart had gotten home in time to light the charcoal grill so that Walter could get the burgers and hot dogs on, and Stephen was already set up to bartend at the kitchen island. Elle had brought a massive green salad for us to share, and Henri and Bear had cleaned out the potato chip aisle. When Pickle and Woody showed up with a watermelon, it felt like we were ready for a full-on barbecue. Marcus had even managed to rustle up a jar of pickles as his contribution, and Rocky had toted along a carafe of decaf for us to drink with dessert.

When Lu came a few minutes later, she had a pitcher of some sort of delicious fruit punch, and I saw Stephen's eyes twinkle as he planned his mixers for the beverage. Mom had told me on our way over that she'd also invited Mindy Washington because she thought she would like to hear what, if anything, Tuck had to share about all the goings on, and I was glad she was coming, even if I still felt a little unclear why Mindy had hidden that book we were looking for.

Still, when Mindy arrived with a huge bowl of the most amazing potato salad I'd ever seen, I decided to let my suspicions go and just enjoy a good night with good friends. And so much good food. So much.

We'd all just made our plates and headed out to join the dogs in the backyard when Tuck and Watson came in. I smiled at them until I saw Reeves come in behind them. My smile quickly fell away as I studied the large man now standing at the edge of my kitchen.

My first instinct was to say, "What is he doing here?" but my Southern manners overruled my candor. Instead, I said, "Nice to see you three. Please help yourselves. We're all going to the backyard."

I wanted to linger to make sure this bully of a man didn't torment Aslan or something, but from her perch on the top of the fridge, I figured Aslan could both protect herself and inflict some serious damage as Reeves passed by, seeing as how his head was within easy paw's reach of her claws.

Stephen stayed inside and poured our latest arrivals their

drinks of choice, and I saw he and Tuck talking briefly over the island. I imagined Stephen was trying to ply him with his punch-infused drink that tasted both like a children's juice box and vanilla cake, and if I knew Tuck, he and Watson were both refusing because they were still on duty. I lost interest in their alcohol-focused tête-à-tête though when I tasted Mindy's potato salad. It was incredible, tangy and just the slightest bit sweet. "Is this celery?" I asked around a mouthful as I pointed to the librarian.

"It is," Mindy said, "and the secret ingredient is turmeric."

"It's so good isn't it?" Lucy said as she waved a forkful of her own in the air.

I couldn't even be bothered to answer because I was so busy savoring the deliciousness.

Once all of us where seated in folding chairs under the lights in the backyard, a semi-comfortable silence descended. I imagined that we were all thinking about the fundraiser last night and also maybe Lippman's signing. I wondered if anyone was as curious as I was to hear what Reeves had told Tuck.

But I didn't have to wonder long because Mom said, "Okay, gentlemen, we've held our tongues long enough. What in the world is going on? We all saw your confab at the store. Spill."

Most everyone looked at Mom with wonder, but I just leaned closer to Tuck as a way of emphasizing Mom's question. I noticed that Marcus and Rocky bent forward, too. If I was too curious, I had friends who ranked right up there with me.

Tuck looked at Stephen and then at Lucy before he answered. "I'm only telling you this because we all need to work together to keep Lucy safe, okay?" He turned his gaze to me. "This information is not an invitation for you to get involved in trying to figure anything out. Understood?"

I wanted to feign innocence, but the mood of the gathering had grown instantly somber. I didn't think making light of things was respectful given Tuck's tone, so I simply nodded.

Tuck continued. "Lucy, forgive me for not talking with you about this privately, but time is of the essence in this situation." He sat forward in his chair. "Is it Joe Cagle you're afraid of?"

Lucy's face blanched, and we had our answer before she even spoke. To her credit, though, she swallowed hard, met Tuck's gaze and said, "Yes."

"I thought so," Reeves said as Tuck met his eyes. "I saw the two of you at the library the day Sidney died. It looked like you were terrified." He stood up and walked over to Lucy before kneeling in the grass in front of her. "I should have said something then. I'm so sorry I didn't."

"You saw him threaten me?" Lucy blinked back tears.

"Is that what he did?" Reeves asked as a flush of purple red spread up his neck and into his face.

Lucy nodded.

"That bas—" Reeves started before Tuck cut him off.

"Lucy, can you please explain the whole story?" Tuck said as he took out his notebook. "We can go inside and talk privately if you'd prefer."

Lucy took a deep breath and shook her head. "No, I think I'd like everyone here to know. You've all been so amazing." She paused and then explained how she'd ended up "dating," a term she used in air quotes, Joe Cagle, and how she'd tried to break it off only to have him threaten her if she did.

"I refused to see him, though, and so he told me he'd tell everyone I was a pedophile." Lucy's voice cracked, and a series of gasps echoed around the yard.

Mindy got up, carried her chair over, and sat down beside Lucy and held her hand. "That's why you tried to destroy the note?"

Lucy said, "Yes, I had kept it as a sort of insurance because I guess some part of me knew that he was shifty or something. But that afternoon when he said he was going to report me to you," she turned to Tuck, "I decided I was going to get rid of the note and just deal with the situation. Maybe move or something."

Mindy shook her head but didn't interrupt.

"But Sidney must have heard me talking on the phone. Joe was yelling, so I guess he could probably have heard him, too, because when I hung up, Sidney looked at me, set his jaw, and forced me to tell him what was going on." Lucy's voice grew quiet. "He was so kind, and it seemed like he was already putting two and two together. So I told him." She broke down. "I put him in danger."

Mart bolted upright in her chair. "No, you did not. Cagle did this, Lucy. Not you. You are not allowed to blame yourself for what he did. You hear me?"

"Right. You are not to blame," I repeated and then listened as first Cate then Elle then Henri and finally Mindy said the same thing. For a brief moment I took the time to appreciate the strong, brave group of women who loved me and who I loved and hoped we could share some of that deep care with Lucy. She so needed it, as we all did.

As Lucy's cries settled, Cate said, "So you told him where he could find the note?"

"I did," Lucy said after taking a deep breath. "He marched right onto the floor to find it. That was the last time I saw him alive." Another deep breath steadied her again as Cate hugged her close.

Tuck cleared his throat. "I hate to ask this, Lucy, but did you see what happened?"

She must have realized that what she was going to say here was crucial because Lucy sat up very straight and said, loud and clear, "I did."

The spiral of emotions inside me was intense. I was thrilled that someone had witnessed Sidney's death and horrified that someone had. I was glad that Lucy could help bring Cagle to justice, and I was terrified for what that meant for her. But none of what I felt mattered. This conversation was what needed to happen, and Lucy looked ready.

"I followed Sidney out, thinking I could help him find the book more quickly. Sidney must have seen the book or something because he went right to it on the sales table. He picked it up, slid the note out, and was about to put the book back when Cagle charged at him out of nowhere. I had been scanning the table around the corner, and I ducked behind the next set of shelves." She put her hand to her heart. "I should have helped him."

Watson slid to the very edge of his seat and said, "No, you did the right thing. You wouldn't have stood a chance, and Cagle would have killed you and Sidney. You did the right thing. You survived."

I studied Deputy Watson's face and saw nothing but compassion there. He was good at this, and I could see why Tuck trusted him with so much.

"Take your time, Lucy," Tuck said. "When you're ready."

Lucy took another deep breath and continued. "Sidney was totally surprised, and Joe must have been much stronger than him because before I knew it, Joe had his hands around Sidney's neck." Lucy rubbed the center of her chest. "It was over before I knew it, and then Joe slid him under the table and started to look around."

"For the note," I said.

Lucy turned her gaze to me. "I think so, but then, he must have heard you coming because he ran around the back of the library past me, but he didn't see me." She sighed. "I'm sorry, but I was so scared."

"You grabbed the note?" Stephen asked.

"Yes. I had seen it slide down beside the boxes of books, and I couldn't risk anyone finding it, especially now." She broke down into tears again. "I'm so sorry."

This time, no one tried to tell her she hadn't made a mistake about the note, but none of us was interested in judging a young woman who had just witnessed the murder of her friend by a man she was involved with.

Cate pulled Lucy to her feet and gave her a big hug just as Henri moved to do the same. The three women held each other tight until Lucy's tears subsided.

As everyone sat back down, I looked at Stephen and then Walter. "Is Cagle at your house?"

"He was when we left," Stephen said. "As far as we know, he hasn't gone anywhere except for walks along the river."

"Obviously, we'd prefer he not be at our house anymore, though," Walter added, and his husband nodded vigorously.

"I will be coming with you to make the arrest," Tuck said. "But if you feel safe, maybe you could go home like you would normally would. I'll just ride along in the back," He turned to Watson, "with you coming up just behind but out of sight."

"To catch him off guard," Watson said.

"I like that plan," Stephen said as he stood. "Are you ready?"

The three other men stood. "We will let you know as soon as we have him in custody," Tuck said to Lucy before turning to me and then Mart. "She's staying with you?"

"Yes," Mart and I said at the same time. "We'll keep her safe," I added.

"Lucas and I will stay, too," Cate said. She turned to Lucy. "If you don't mind sharing a bed, I'll sleep with you, and Lucas can take the couch."

I smiled and said, "I like that plan. It'll be like a sleepover."

Lucy smiled. "Sounds good. I don't have anything to sleep in or a toothbrush or anything."

"We've got you covered, all of you," Mart said to our friends.

Stephen, Walter, Tuck, and Watson were already on their way to the door, and I prayed this arrest was simple and straightforward with no surprises. When Reeves said a quick thank you and followed them out, I felt a little pang of guilt that

I had judged him so harshly. I didn't understand why he hadn't talked to Tuck right away, but maybe he thought he could handle things on his own. I certainly understood that impulse.

The rest of our friends helped us clean up, and then they headed to their cars and went on home after getting our assurances that we'd keep them posted as soon as we heard anything. Mom and Dad took a little extra convincing that we'd be okay. Dad even offered to sleep in his car, but I urged them to trust Tuck and go home and get some rest.

Despite the fact that we'd all had a very busy two days and an incredibly stressful week, I knew that none of us would be able to sleep just yet. So we turned on the TV and forced Lucas to watch *Shadow and Bone*, the TV series based on the books that all the women in the room had loved. Playing along, Lucas critiqued the romance, the special effects, and the boat-building techniques for the first few minutes, but before long, we were all engrossed and cheering for Alina and Mal as they crossed the Fold.

We got so engrossed in the show that we didn't realize until the end of the episode, almost an hour later that we hadn't heard from Tuck yet. I grabbed my phone, hoping that it had just been set to silent. But there was nothing.

After checking his phone, too, Lucas didn't hesitate and called Tuck's cell. The sheriff answered on the first ring. "He's not there," we all heard him say over the speaker. "We've organized a manhunt. Lock everything down and stay put." Then, he hung up.

Lucy snuggled closer to Cate on the couch, and I had to really resist the temptation to squeeze into the club chair with Mart. Instead, she and I got up and double-checked the doors and windows, which were all securely locked. Then, I sat down in front of Mayhem, Taco, and Sasquatch for their pep talk. "Dogs, we need you to alert us if you hear anything, anything at all. Can you do that?"

All of them studied my face for a minute and then laid their heads back down on their beds. I noticed, though, that none of them closed their eyes. They knew something was up.

On Mart's suggestion, we decided to all sleep in the living room and we gathered all the blankets and pillows in the house to make as soft a pallet as we could for our bodies. I was going to regret sleeping on the floor in the morning, but not as much as I'd regret my choice to sleep in my bed if something happened to anyone here.

Lucas had let all of our friends know what was going on, and while he had assured them all that we were fine and taking good care, it wasn't long before a pajama-clad train of people came knocking at the door. Even Symeon, Mart's boyfriend, came over now that his shift at Max's restaurant was over.

Only Stephen and Walter didn't return because they were on the hunt for Cagle with Tuck, Watson, and the officers they'd brought in from surrounding police forces. If it wasn't so terrifying, these events might have been exciting in a "true crime" book kind of way.

Mart got Cate and Lucy some of our T-shirts and pajama pants and brought Taco back to stay with them while they changed. I didn't know if the Basset would do anything if there was danger, but I certainly expected him to sound the alarm.

After Bear and Pickle did a thorough search of the house and checked all the doors and windows again, we all settled into the pile of blankets and pillows in the living room. Because he had a bad back, Bear took the couch, and somehow, Henri managed to curl up next to him. Lucas stretched his long, lean frame out in one of the club chairs, and Woody made himself a pallet of the dog beds and a blanket while the three pups curled against him to steal his body heat.

The rest of us sorted ourselves into some levels of comfort on the floor, and I was grateful for Aslan's presence at my feet, especially since I knew this wasn't her ideal sleeping moment.

She liked to have a lot of room available, even if she insisted on squeezing into the crevices my body created as I slept.

By silent agreement, we all decided to try to get to sleep, a feat which was going to be very hard given the circumstances and the sleeping arrangements. I calmed my nerves using a strategy I'd built as a child and thought through all the things that were between us and the man who wanted to hurt one of us. The police, the dozen cars out front, the house itself, the people around us. At some point, I dozed off to the soft breaths of the people I loved, and while I didn't exactly feel at ease, I did feel comforted, protected.

SOMETIME IN THE darkest part of the night, I was jarred awake by Aslan's claws digging into my calf. I sat up and looked down at her, and she was ready to pounce as she looked down the hall. I glanced over at where the dogs had been curled against Woody and saw that they were up and staring the same direction as the cat. Something was going on down there.

I texted Tuck and then nudged Mom and Mart awake and pointed to the animals. Mayhem's hackles were up now, so she was definitely about to charge. Dad took hold of her collar and grabbed Taco's, too just as Cate hugged Sasquatch to her chest. If Cagle was in this house, I wasn't about to let him hurt my dogs.

Mom went around and woke everyone and put her fingers to her lips every time a pair of eyes opened. Our best bet was the element of surprise, especially if Cagle thought he was catching us unawares.

I didn't like guns and neither did Mart, so we didn't allow them in our house. But we did have fireplace pokers and knives, so as silently as we could, Mart and I armed everyone, and then we waited.

As we all sat stock-still, I heard the sound that must have

tipped off my pets – a slight creaking that reminded me of the way tree branches sound in the wind. The sound continued for a few moments more, and then I heard a splintering crack followed by the quick woosh that was clearly a window opening. The jerk had broken one of our window locks.

Cate stepped in front of Lucy just as the first footfall sounded in Mart's bedroom. Cagle must have presumed we'd be asleep in the beds at the back, but there's no way he could have known which room Lucy would be in. I could only hope that when he found an empty bed, he didn't head toward the front of the house rather than checking the other rooms. We were ready, but I really didn't want us to need our readiness.

Fortunately, Cagle didn't come our way before going into my room and then, more loudly, into the guest bedroom. He was taking less care to be quiet, and I wondered if he thought we weren't there. A tiny spark of hope ignited in my chest. Maybe he would just go back out the way he came.

My hope sputtered out when the sound of footsteps came down the hall. He wasn't doing anything at all to be quiet now, so I had to assume he really did think we were gone. For a split second, I wondered if we could all hide, duck behind the kitchen island and couch and just wait him out. But given that our house had an open-concept floor plan, there really wasn't anywhere that couldn't be seen from the rest of the room. And even if there had been, we were out of time. Cagle was striding right toward where we huddled beside the fireplace.

It took him a minute to see us since we were massed together in a darker corner of the room, but when he did, a grin broke out across his face. And it wasn't a nice grin either. I had a momentary memory of the way Skeletor looked in the old He-Man cartoon. But then, Cagle spoke. "Lucy, there you are. I was so worried about you."

Behind me, Lucy whimpered.

Lucas stepped forward with Henri beside him and Bear

right with them. Pickle and Elle pushed in beside Cate, Symeon, Mart, and me so that we could shield Lucy against the wall. Mom and Dad took wide-legged stances in front of me, and I saw Woody inching his way toward the kitchen. Cagle was going to have to fight through all of us, and we were going to put up a hell of a fight.

"Go home, Cagle," Henri said as she took another step forward.

Beside me I saw the faint light of a cellphone flicker on and noted that Mart was typing a message into the screen with her phone tucked behind her thigh. Her texting skills were always so amazing.

"I'm just here to be sure Lucy is all right. I know that man Reeves is following her, and I want to be sure she's safe." Cagle's voice was soft and gentle, but he was walking closer and closer to us.

"She's fine," I said with as much strength as I could mount up over my fear. "As you can see, we are all making sure she's safe. Now, please leave."

Cagle took another step closer. "I see that you all want to keep her safe, but if I can break into your house so easily, so can Reeves." He leaned forward so that he was almost touching Pickle's chest with outstretched hands. "Lucy, I will take care of you, darling. That's my job."

I felt Lucy shudder behind me as she slipped her face between my shoulder and Mart's. "No, it's not. It's my job to take care of myself, and these people are my friends. I am staying here."

Even in the darkness, I could see something like rage flash in Cagle's eyes. He looked from Pickle to Lucas to Henri to Woody, and then he must have decided his odds were good because he charged forward like a wolf who has trapped his prey.

He didn't get far though because Lucas clotheslined him as

he tried to run by, and I almost cheered. Woody cleared the last few feet from behind the couch and grabbed his legs. Then Pickle put a foot on his chest and Henri brandished a bread knife and stood over him with daring in her face.

"There's rope at the back door," Mart said as we all began to move, and Elle and Woody grabbed the rope Mart had bought for us to use for our clothesline and hogtied Cagle.

Meanwhile, Lucy, Cate, and I turned toward Lucy and grabbed her just before she fainted. The three of us managed to carry her to the couch, and I was just putting a cold washcloth on her face when our front door blew open.

Reeves was plowing through the door with Tuck, Watson, Stephen, and Walter just behind him. Tuck had his gun drawn, and Reeves' hands were balled into fists. Even Stephen and Walter, who didn't believe in violence, looked set and ready for a fight.

But when Reeves caught site of Lucy on the couch, he sank to his knees. Tuck holstered his weapon, and Stephen and Walter moved into the room.

Cate and Mart continued to talk with Lucy as she came to, and I moved over to let Tuck know exactly what had happened. As I described Cagle's break-in and his systematic movement through the house, I heard Reeves swearing under his breath behind me. "I should have come in sooner," he said to himself.

I turned. "You were outside this whole time?"

Reeves blushed. "I wanted to be sure Lucy was safe" was all he said.

I studied his face for a few seconds, but all I saw there was a mixture of concern and fear as he looked at the young woman on the sofa.

"Did anyone get hurt?" Watson asked as he put a hand on my arm.

I tried to ignore the tingle of sensation that ran up to my neck from his touch and said, "No. Everyone is fine." I smiled as best I could, but I wasn't sure my facial muscles were working quite right. The adrenaline was wearing off, and I felt like I could actually join Lucy on the couch if I wasn't careful.

"Sit down, Harvey," Mom said, and for once, I listened and dropped into a club chair just as Mart sat down on my lap. "I'll get you both some tea."

How my mother could still function after all this stress and lack of sleep was a mystery to me, but I let her because I didn't think I could walk, much less safely carry a cup of something hot around the room.

Soon, though, Tuck and Watson had taken Cagle back to the station, this time after reading him his rights, and the rest of us had settled in with tea, some of us with something a little stronger mixed in. I took a double dose of stronger when Dad offered.

Stephen and Walter asked if we'd mind telling them what happened, and Mart obliged. "So he broke in and then went room by room to find—?" Walter stopped himself when he saw how wan Lucy still looked on the couch.

I nodded. "He was very intent."

"Obsessed," Reeves said from his stool by the island. "He was obsessed."

"Clearly," Cate said quietly. "Are you okay, Lucy?"

She nodded and took another sip of her stronger tea, a special blend of mostly not tea that Dad had mixed up for her to calm her nerves. Chamomile and whiskey seemed to be helping.

I couldn't disagree with Reeves, but I did have one question. "You were just outside all night, waiting?" I asked him.

He nodded. "In my truck. I just had a bad feeling, but I didn't want to intrude or make anyone more nervous." He ran his fingers through his hair. "I'm sorry I scared you all with how intense I was about finding Cagle."

"Someone might say you were a bit obsessed yourself," Lucas said with a smile.

"They might indeed," Reeves said with a long look at Lucy. "I better go on home. I have a pair of kittens who will miss me if I don't."

The thought of this huge man with little kittens was just so incongruous that I couldn't help but smile, even as I did wonder, not for the first time, what exactly had made Reeves care so very much.

I was too tired to think about it, though, and soon I drifted off in my chair.

14

I woke up with sunshine full in my face and the voices of my friends whispering around me. As I opened my eyes and stretched the crick out of my neck, I smiled. Apparently everyone had stayed and slept in various positions around the room. Only Lucy looked restful since she had slept on the couch. The rest of us, and I'm sure me included, looked like we'd been in bar fights that left us with circles under our eyes and rats' nests for hair.

Fortunately, Rocky and Marcus each responded immediately when I saw it was almost nine-thirty. They were already at the store and ready to open on time. "Left something for you on the front stoop," Rocky's message added. "Get there before the dogs."

I looked over to where Mayhem, Taco, Sasquatch, and Aslan were curled up by the fireplace in some sort of excitement-induced camaraderie and thought, *No problem. Those guys aren't going anywhere for a while.*

When I opened the door, I whooped with delight. There, Rocky had left a carafe of coffee and a box of cinnamon rolls.

The note said, "Tuck filled us in first thing. Come in whenever" in Rocky's beautiful handwriting.

I didn't even wait before shoving a cinnamon roll in my mouth. When I turned back to the room with a cinnamon roll hanging out of my lips, the laughter that broke out was so infectious, I almost dropped my breakfast. Fortunately, Mart saved me and got the box and coffee from my hands just in time for me to catch the rest of the deliciousness before Taco got to it. That dog could go from dead asleep to wide awake at the slightest scent of food.

As we all ate, I texted Mindy to let her know what had happened and ask, at Lucy's sleepy request, if Lucy could come in that afternoon to talk with her boss. Mindy agreed readily, and I knew that she was going to make a great new director for the library, even if the decision hadn't been formally made yet.

My friends and I chatted about the songbirds outside and our plans for the backyard and landscaping around the house. Elle made suggestions about good plants to include, and Woody offered to build us a bench for the back corner under the red maple. The conversation stayed light as if by some unspoken agreement we all knew we needed some time to process the events of the night before.

Lucy seemed okay this morning, but Walter and Stephen insisted on driving her home, a gift that she tried to refused but only half-heartedly. Pickle headed out to step down as Cagle's lawyer because, obviously, he had a conflict of interest now. "Hard to defend a man well when he threatened you and your friends," he said on his way out.

Slowly, the rest of us put the living room back together and drank the rest of the coffee, and then our friends headed on their way to their own jobs and businesses. It was going to be a sleep-deprived day around St. Marin's, but it was a weekend at the beginning of the tourist season. None of us could afford to take the day off.

After everyone had left, Mart and I both got showers, and after I assured her I wanted to walk into work and that Taco and Mayhem would definitely alert someone if I collapsed on the way, she drove off to her wine tasting event at a nearby horse farm. Mayhem, always the more attuned of the pair of my dogs, set the pace easy and light as we walked down the streets of town in time to see cars with people in pastel church clothes headed out. Some of my neighbors were pulling weeds or trimming hedges, and everyone waved. It would have felt like an idyllic Sunday morning if I had been able to shake the lingering anxiety from the night before.

I'd finally learned from my experiences and that I had to let myself feel what I felt and trust that I'd come through it when I had braved the darkness. So I let myself cry a little as I turned onto the Main Street and took a loop up by Elle's shop, where she was opening the door with a bunch of orange daylilies in hand. She smiled and nodded as I wiped a tear away and waved.

Cate gave me a big – if tired – smile as I walked past her studio at the art co-op. The lobby was full of guests, and I knew that even though she was exhausted, Cate was excited that the artists she supported were getting some attention. I hoped Henri's studio was full of art lovers who were buying her weavings, too.

Max's restaurant was packed with his in-season brunch crowd, and Symeon was outside baking pizzas in the street-side oven he'd built. I smiled as I passed by and said, "That smells so good" in my most enthusiastic voice with a wish that he'd get a huge number of pizza orders for the afternoon. Inside, I saw Max and Mel talking in a quiet corner.

My store was buzzing, too, and as I unhooked Mayhem and Taco, I glanced around. Marcus had redone the front tables, leaving a small section for the remaining copies of Lippman's books that we still had and adding in a whole slew of thriller titles to flesh out the display. He'd even made a sign that said, "If you love Laura Lippman, you'll love these thrillers, too." I was particularly happy that he'd featured *The Only Good Indians* by Stephen Graham Jones because the book was so creepy and because the cover was gorgeous. From the looks of it, the books were already selling, and I made a note to order in more thrillers since they were great vacation reads.

After checking in with Marcus and learning that nothing special needed my attention in the shop, I headed over for my latte and to thank Rocky for the thoughtful gift. "It was nothing," she said. "Sounded like you all had a hard night? Sorry we weren't there."

I shook my head. "I'm not. We need at least two people in town who aren't too sleep-deprived to make good decisions."

Rocky laughed. "Well, if anyone needs us to weigh in, I'm sure I can speak for Marcus and say we're happy to help." She glanced over at her boyfriend, who winked at her. They were simply so sweet together.

I spent the next hour or so keeping myself upright by tidying shelves and pulling down backstock. Marcus managed the customer end of things for both of us since I wasn't sure I could recall the titles of books, much less make good recommendations.

About noon, Tuck came in, and I pointed toward the wingback chairs in the fiction section to suggest we talk there, a suggestion that also gave both of us a chance to rest. Even walking around, I was having a little trouble keeping my eyes open. It looked like I was going to need to make an exception to my no caffeine after noon rule.

I smiled at my friend as he sat down even more heavily than I did. "Did you get any sleep?"

"Not yet," he said. "But I'm headed home after I talk with you. Lu's orders."

"Good woman," I said. "You don't owe me information, though, Tuck. Just go on home."

Tuck smiled. "I know I don't *owe* you anything, Harvey, but I want to give you an update and then ask that you let everyone know. You all probably saved Lucy's life last night, so I thought you'd all be interested to know that Cagle has been charged with Sidney's murder."

I sighed. "Good. That's good," I said quietly. "Did he confess?"

Tuck shook his head. "And I don't think he will. He's too far deep into his role as Lucy's protector to think he did anything wrong at all, but he's also too smart to say too much."

"But you have enough evidence." I tried to sound very confident in my friend, but I knew that enough sometimes isn't.

"The district attorney assures me that the case in iron-clad since Lucy has already agreed to testify to what she saw. Between that and Cagle's breaking and entering, we have got it, Harvey." Tuck rubbed his chin. "I just wish we could also get him for what he did to Lucy before . . ."

"Yeah, me too." I took a deep breath and asked, "Do you know why Reeves was so invested in keeping Lucy safe? I mean he saw one interchange and took it on himself to protect her."

Tuck sighed and nodded. "He told me about his daughter who had been assaulted by her boyfriend. He had ignored the warning signs, and he still feels guilty."

I blew air out of my pursed lips. "So when he saw Lucy and Cagle arguing . . ."

"Yep. He didn't want to wait to act this time."

We sat quietly for a few minutes, but then I felt pressed to say something. "Tuck, you are a good sheriff, you know that, right?"

Tuck looked up and met my gaze. His eyes grew soft, and he said, "Thank you, Harvey. Most days, I think I do my job well, but some days . . ."

"Some days, we all need to be reminded of our worth," I said quietly. "As you ramp up your campaign, let me know how I can help, okay?"

He stood and offered a hand to pull me up. "Will do, Harvey. Will do." He looked over at the café. "Now, go get the latte Rocky is waving in the air before you fall asleep standing up."

I laughed and made my way over to the café. The mug Rocky handed me was the size of a soup bowl, and I didn't hesitate. "Full strength? I asked as I took a long pull from the hot liquid.

"Of course," Rocky said. "Just like you."

HARVEY AND MARCUS'S BOOK RECOMMENDATIONS

Here, you will find all the books and authors recommended in *Proof Of Death* to add to your never-ending to-read-list!

- *The Storied Life of AJ Fikry* by Gabrielle Zevin
- *The Dragon and the Ghost* by Mark Dawson
- *The Angel* by Mark Dawson
- *Death of a Gossip* by M.C. Beaton
- *Stiff* by Mary Roach
- *The Midnight Library* by Matt Haig
- *Black Sun* by Rebecca Roanhorse
- *The Cracked Spine* by Paige Shelton
- *The Library of Lost and Found* by Phaedra Parick
- *The Bean Trees* by Barbara Kingsolver
- *Ender's Game* by Orson Scott Card
- *The Overstory* by Richard Powers
- *Braiding Sweetgrass* by Robin Kimmerer Wall
- *Shades In Shadow* by N.K. Jemisin
- *The End of Policing* by Alex S. Vitale
- *Mindhunter* by John E. Douglas

- *A Day at the Police Station* by Richard Scary
- *The Hidden Life of Trees* by Peter Wohlleben
- *Caraval* by Stephen Garber
- *The Long Fall* by Walter Mosley
- *Another Thing to Fall* by Laura Lippman
- *The River Has Teeth* by Erica Waters
- *Midnight at the Great Ideas Bookstore* by Matthew Sullivan
- *African American Poetry: 250 Years of Struggle* edited by Kevin Young
- *Slow Samson* by Bethany Christou
- *Rules for Being a Girl* by Candice Bushnell and Katie Cotugno
- *Pride* by Ibi Zoboi
- *The Plot Is Murder* by VM Burns
- *Belly Button Book* by Sandra Boynton
- *Rapunzel* by Paul O. Zelinksy
- *Ramona* by Beverly Cleary
- *I Was Told There'd Be Cake* by Sloane Crosby
- *The Solace of Open Spaces* by Gretel Ehrlich
- *My Life as a Villainess* by Laura Lippman
- *Odd Thomas* by Dean Koontz
- *The Westing Game* by Ellen Raskin
- *Wilde Lake* by Laura Lippman
- *The Hairstons* by Henri Wiencek
- *The Only Good Indians* by Stephen Graham Jones

I recommend these books highly. Feel free to drop me a line at acfbookens@andilit.com and let me know if you read any or have books you think I should read. Thanks!

Happy Reading,
ACF

WANT TO READ ABOUT HARVEY'S FIRST SLEUTHING EXPEDITION?

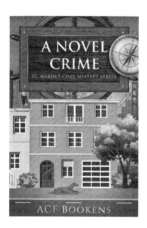

Join my Cozy Up email group for weekly book recs & a FREE copy of *A Novel Crime*, the prequel to the St. Marin's Cozy Mystery Series.

Sign-up here - https://bookens.andilit.com/CozyUp

ALSO BY ACF BOOKENS

St. Marin's Cozy Mystery Series

Publishable By Death

Entitled To Kill

Bound To Execute

Plotted For Murder

Tome To Tomb

Scripted To Slay

Epilogue Of An Epitaph - Coming October 2021

Stitches In Crime Series

Crossed By Death

Bobbins and Bodies

Hanged By A Thread

Counted Corpse - Coming August 2021

ABOUT THE AUTHOR

ACF Bookens lives in the Southwest Mountains of Virginia, where the mountain tops remind her that life is a rugged beauty of a beast worthy of our attention. When she's not writing, she enjoys chasing her son around the house with the full awareness she will never catch him, cross-stitching while she binge-watches police procedurals, and reading everything she can get her hands on. Find her at bookens.andilit.com.

 facebook.com/bookenscozymysteries

Made in the USA
Columbia, SC
09 May 2022

60175224R00102